Kylee

Cap 4t

*Reality Check*

LOOK FOR THE OTHER BOOKS IN THIS
INSPIRATIONAL NEW SERIES,
COMING SOON FROM BANTAM BOOKS.

#3 *Heart & Soul*

#4 *Promises, Promises*

AND DON'T MISS THE FIRST BOOK IN THE
SERIES, *Get a Life.*

# clearwater crossing

# Reality Check

## laura peyton roberts

BANTAM BOOKS
NEW YORK • TORONTO • LONDON • SYDNEY • AUCKLAND

RL 5.8, age 12 and up
REALITY CHECK
A Bantam Book/April 1998

All scripture quotations, unless otherwise indicated, are taken from
the HOLY BIBLE, NEW INTERNATIONAL VERSION®. NIV®.
Copyright © 1973, 1978, 1984 by International Bible Society. Used by
permission of Zondervan Publishing House. All rights reserved.

All rights reserved.
Copyright © 1998 by Laura Peyton Roberts.
Cover photography by Michael Segal.
Cover art copyright © 1998 by Bantam Doubleday Dell
Books for Young Readers.
No part of this book may be reproduced or transmitted
in any form or by any means, electronic or mechanical,
including photocopying, recording, or by any information
storage and retrieval system, without permission in
writing from the publisher.

If you purchased this book without a cover you should be aware
that this book is stolen property. It was reported as "unsold and
destroyed" to the publisher, and neither the author nor the
publisher has received any payment for this "stripped book."

ISBN 0-553-57121-4

Published simultaneously in the United States and Canada.

Bantam Books are published by Bantam Books, a division of Bantam
Doubleday Dell Publishing Group, Inc. Its trademark, consisting of the
words "Bantam Books" and the portrayal of a rooster, is Registered in
U.S. Patent and Trademark Office and in other countries. Marca Reg-
istrada. Bantam Books, 1540 Broadway, New York, New York 10036.

PRINTED IN THE UNITED STATES OF AMERICA

CWO     10  9  8  7  6  5  4  3  2  1

*For Dick, my husband and best friend*

So we fix our eyes not on what is seen, but on what is unseen. For what is seen is temporary, but what is unseen is eternal.

2 Corinthians 4:18

# One

"There you are!" Leah Rosenthal called, relieved, as Miguel del Rios drove up and parked his battered old clunker near the corner. She checked her wristwatch distractedly—10:50 Saturday morning. "I was starting to think I was waiting in the wrong place."

"Sorry." Miguel got out of the car and slammed the door behind him. "I . . . uh . . . got held up. Did you bring a hammer?"

"I thought *you* were bringing the hammer!" Leah cried, her hazel eyes widening. How were they supposed to put up the signs for the Eight Prime car wash without a hammer? It was too late to go home and get one—she and Miguel were supposed to meet the rest of the group in Clearwater Crossing Park at eleven. *I told Miguel we ought to start with the signs at ten, but he said ten-thirty was early enough. And now he's late. . . .*

"We agreed that *I'd* make the signs and *you'd* nail them up, remember?"

"No. Are you sure?"

1

"Miguel!" She was on the verge of panicking when he broke into an irresistibly handsome grin.

"You're so cute when you're serious," he teased. "Of *course* I brought the hammer." He flipped a screwdriver out of his back pocket and started walking toward the trunk of his car. "I brought two, in fact. How many signs did you make?"

"Ten for phone poles and two more for the parking lot," she answered, pointing to the pile on the sidewalk. "And I think you're horrible to joke about something so important." She attempted to look put out, but it was a wasted effort. The truth was that she was so happy to see him, she'd forgiven him the second he'd driven up.

Miguel popped open his trunk, using the screwdriver in the broken lock. "But horrible in a good way, right?" His brown eyes sparkled, and his smile flashed white against his tan as he handed her a hammer.

"No, just horrible." Leah tried to make her face severe, but the corners of her eyes crinkled in a renegade smile that answered his. "Are we going to hang these signs, or what?" she asked, turning to walk away.

Miguel caught her by the wrist and pulled her into his arms. "What's the hurry?"

His handsome face was only inches from hers. It would have been so easy to put her arms around him, to forget about the car wash, to kiss him right there in Clearwater Boulevard traffic. . . .

"Stop it, Miguel," she said, reluctantly pushing him away. "Someone will see us."

"I don't care."

"Yes, you do. And so do I." Neither one of them had told anyone they were dating yet, and Leah had envisioned a more dignified way of letting people know. "Besides, we're already late. We have to get these signs up, then go help wash cars."

"Work, work, work," Miguel grumbled, letting her go, but the smile on his face made it clear he was kidding. "Okay, *mein commandant.*" He snapped to attention and saluted her with the other hammer, pretending to smack himself in the forehead in the process. He staggered around the sidewalk like a bad Charlie Chaplin imitator, trying to make her believe it had hurt.

"You're insane," Leah told him, an amazed smile on her face. She could barely believe this was the same shy guy she'd had to fight to get two words out of only the week before.

"No. I'm happy."

The way he looked at her when he said it nearly took Leah's breath away.

"I can't believe you signed up to spend a beautiful Saturday like this washing cars," Nicole Brewster's best friend, Courtney Bell, complained as

Nicole drove them down Clearwater Boulevard toward the park. "Are you completely crazy?"

*I must be,* Nicole thought sarcastically. *I brought you.* She'd had her reservations about asking Courtney to help, and she was starting to think they'd been justified. So far all Courtney had done was complain—that and make fun of Nicole for agreeing to be part of Eight Prime.

The fall semester had barely begun, and already Clearwater Crossing High School had suffered a major tragedy. Kurt Englbehrt, a well-liked senior, had survived leukemia only to be killed in a car accident a few days after his remission was announced. The entire town was still reeling from the shock. Just two weekends before, Nicole had worked at a carnival to raise money to help pay Kurt's medical bills. She and seven other student volunteers—Leah Rosenthal, Miguel del Rios, Jenna Conrad, Peter Altmann, Ben Pipkin, Melanie Andrews, and Jesse Jones—had cooked hamburgers and served lemonade to advance that good cause.

Of course, the cause Nicole had been more interested in at the time was getting Jesse Jones to like her, but that was ancient history now. Kurt's death had rocked her, and Jesse had turned out to be human slime in a football jersey. Only the friendship of some of the other members of her carnival team had kept Nicole from despairing completely. She could hardly say no when they asked her to join them in raising money to buy a bus for the Junior Explorers—an underprivileged children's program— to donate in Kurt's memory. Not even if it *did* mean spending more time around Jesse and pain-in- the-butt Melanie Andrews, the perfect sophomore cheerleader Jesse worshiped. The temporary group the eight of them had formed had become known as Eight Prime.

"You said you didn't have anything better to do today, Courtney," Nicole reminded her friend. "Be- sides, the sooner we earn this stupid bus, the sooner I can be through with these people."

"A worthy goal," Courtney replied with a smirk. "But this is a one-time thing for me, Nicole. Don't expect to drag me on your little fund-raisers every weekend."

"Don't worry. I won't."

Her tone made Courtney shoot her a suspicious look, but then the tree-shaded entrance to the parking lot came into view. "Look at all those little kids!" Courtney groaned. "We're going to end up *baby-sitting!*"

"I told you the kids were going to help too." But to herself Nicole had to admit she hadn't realized there would be so many of them—the parking lot was a zoo! Several members of Eight Prime milled about on the asphalt, along with a bunch of ram- bunctious first- and second-graders Nicole could only assume were Junior Explorers.

"Whoa! Who's *that?*" Courtney asked suddenly, sitting up straighter in the passenger seat as the car rolled slowly through the crowded parking lot.

Nicole shook her head. "I don't know." The tall, brown-haired guy Courtney was gawking at was head-turningly handsome and too old to be in high school. Even with a swarm of little kids hanging on his arms and clinging to his muscular brown legs, he still managed to look cool. "Maybe that's Chris Hobart, Peter's partner in the Junior Explorers."

At the mention of Peter Altmann, Courtney rolled her eyes. "I suppose it's too much to hope that the God Squad didn't come today," she said, checking her hair in the rearview mirror. Peter and his best friend, Jenna, had been in a class with Courtney the year before, and she'd taken an immediate dislike to them because of their overt Christianity. As far as Courtney was concerned, having a religion was stupid—discussing it in public was unforgivable. The fact that Nicole attended church every Sunday did nothing to change Courtney's mind—or shut her mouth.

"Courtney . . . ," Nicole warned.

"Oh, all right. I said I'd be nice to them, didn't I?"

The girls climbed out of the car and unloaded the folding card table and cash box Nicole had brought, then began walking back toward the crowd at the entrance to the parking lot. The scent of freshly mown grass hung in the warm morning air, and Nicole wished briefly that she'd worn shorts instead of jeans, like Courtney. At least her top was cute—a knit vest over a blue T-shirt and white tank top. She could always take off a layer or two later if it got too hot.

They approached the grass at the edge of the lot, where everything the other members of Eight Prime had volunteered to bring was already laid out. Hoses, buckets, towels, soap in squeeze bottles, and brightly colored sponges littered the shady area. Nicole headed instinctively toward the chaos, Courtney tagging along behind.

"Nicole! Hi!" Jenna called, trotting over to them. Her thick brown hair was pulled back in a high ponytail, and, like Nicole, she wore jeans. "Let me give you a hand with that!"

Jenna helped carry the card table to the grass, where they unfolded it under a big oak tree. Nicole set the rusted old cash box her father had given her on top.

"Great! You got the box," Jenna said happily. She opened the creaking lid to look inside. "And starter change! We should count how much money is in here so we can pay you back afterward."

"Actually, that's my parents' donation to the cause," Nicole explained. "They said we should keep it, along with the box."

Courtney suddenly cleared her throat, interrupting the conversation.

"Oh," said Nicole, startled by the not-so-subtle hint. "Jenna, do you remember Courtney? I think you two had a class together last year."

Jenna gave Courtney a friendly smile. "English, right? I thought you looked familiar."

"Yeah. You and your friend Peter always sat in the front row."

"That's right," Jenna said, as if flattered that Courtney remembered. She apparently didn't realize that in Courtney's scheme of reality only dweebs sat in the front. Luckily, they were interrupted just then by a junior-high–age girl with an unruly mass of long auburn curls and an atomic explosion of freckles.

"Jenna!" she cried, excitedly running up to them. "Peter said to tell you that Leah and Miguel are done with the signs and we're going to start flagging in cars."

"Okay." Jenna turned to introduce her. "Maggie, meet Nicole and Courtney. This is my sister Maggie. Where's Caitlin?" she asked the girl.

"With Maura. I'm going to go help Peter." Maggie was off as quickly as she'd arrived, her freckled white legs propelling her back toward the street.

"Who's Caitlin?" asked Nicole.

"Another sister. There's six of us altogether, but only five still living at home. Listen, I'd better go hear what Peter's plan is," Jenna added. "Talk to you later."

Nicole and Courtney watched as Jenna strode off across the thick green lawn in the direction Maggie had gone.

"Six kids," Courtney said disgustedly. "Like the world isn't crowded enough already!"

"It is kind of a lot," Nicole agreed reluctantly. She liked Jenna. She wished Courtney would get off her case.

An ear-splitting whistle cut through the park. Nicole and Courtney spun around in time to see Peter take both index fingers out of his mouth and start waving everyone over.

"I guess we're starting now," said Nicole.

"Yippee," Courtney replied.

Nicole couldn't admit it to Courtney, but she wasn't entirely thrilled about the whole thing herself. She didn't mind washing cars, but the closer they got to the group, the closer they got to her two new enemies: Jesse Jones and Melanie Andrews. She could see them now, hanging back on the fringes together as the rest of Eight Prime and the Junior Explorers pressed in closer to listen to Peter. Melanie looked as picture-perfect as always in pleated white shorts and a sleeveless madras blouse, and Jesse looked cute enough to be dangerous even in grungy old cutoffs.

*It doesn't matter,* Nicole told herself. *I'm going to ignore him, no matter what. My mind's made up to—*

"You didn't tell me Miguel del Rios was part of

9

this bus thing!" Courtney said suddenly in an excited whisper.

"Huh? Oh. I guess it didn't occur to me. I didn't know you knew him."

"Please! *Everybody* knows him. The guy's a total babe!"

"Look, do me a favor and don't hit on Miguel," Nicole begged as they approached the group. "I've got to be able to face these people again next week."

Courtney smiled. "I'll grant your wish, but only because I'm already busy with Jeff tonight. Otherwise there's no way I'd promise you something so selfish."

Nicole winced at the mention of *selfish*. She knew Courtney was only kidding, but she also knew she'd been way too self-involved lately—it was the main reason she'd joined Eight Prime in the first place.

"Anyway, I'm glad to know there are some normal people here too," Courtney added. "At least not *everyone* in the group is a dork."

She was looking at Melanie and Jesse when she said it, Nicole noticed, although Courtney obviously meant to include Chris and Miguel in the not-a-dork category too. It irritated Nicole that her best friend would have *anything* nice to say about Melanie Andrews—even that she wasn't a dork—when she knew Nicole was planning to ignore

Melanie and Jesse as much as possible. And even though Courtney didn't agree that Melanie was responsible for Jesse's unforgivable behavior, Nicole thought her friend should support her.

"Okay!" Peter called, waving one hand overhead for attention. "Let's get this show on the road!" People crowded in closer to hear his instructions.

"Chris and the Junior Explorers are going to be walking up and down the grass at the edge of Clearwater Boulevard to attract attention and wave cars into the parking lot. When the cars come in, try to make them line up where we can reach them with the hoses."

"Are we going to work in teams?" Ben Pipkin asked. Nicole glanced at Ben in his baggy plaid Bermudas, then looked quickly away, refusing to meet Courtney's eyes. He was actually a pretty nice guy, but the way he dressed was embarrassing. Nicole could imagine Courtney's mental calculator working overtime to subtract all the not-a-dork points she'd awarded the group only moments before.

"I don't think we need to assign teams," Peter replied, pushing back his dark blond hair. "Everyone just pitch in wherever. Remember, we're washing the whole outside and cleaning both sides of the windows. When a car is finished, someone who worked on it should collect five dollars and either put it in the cash box or keep it to turn in later. Is everybody ready?"

11

"I can barely wait," Courtney muttered under cover of a cheer from the Junior Explorers.

"Okay, guys," Peter told the kids. "Get out there and start bringing in cars!"

"Hey, Jenna, toss me one of those sponges, would you?" Peter called. She and Ben were on the other side of a Cadillac the three of them were washing. Jenna fished a pink one out of her bucket and threw it over the roof.

"Hey!" The sponge hit Peter in the shoulder, exploding in a burst of dirty water that soaked his emerald green T-shirt and splashed him across the face. He rubbed his eyes with both hands, trying to clear out the soap suds.

"You *said* to throw it," Jenna reminded him quickly, before he could get mad.

Ben chuckled beside her, and even Peter had to smile. He bent to pick the sponge up off the pavement, then fired it back at Jenna over the top of the car.

"Peter!" she squealed, ducking just in time. The sponge whizzed over her head. "What are you doing?"

"I can't use it after it's been on the ground," he said innocently. "You have to rinse it out again."

"Uh-uh! You were trying to hit me!"

"That would have been a bonus," Peter admitted, a mischievous glint in his eyes.

Jenna rinsed out the sponge and handed it carefully to her friend, happy that the car wash was going so well. Everyone in Eight Prime was scrubbing away like crazy, and Chris Hobart and his girlfriend, Maura, were marching all but a few of the Junior Explorers up and down the grass at the edge of Clearwater Boulevard. The kids marched enthusiastically, brandishing the signs Chris and Peter had helped them make earlier that morning, when the two counselors had explained about the new bus. Most of the signs were illegible, and many of them featured crayon drawings of strange, futuristic vehicles unlike any bus Jenna had ever seen, but the passersby were getting the idea anyway, thanks to Leah's carefully lettered boards.

Jenna looked up from washing the butter yellow Cadillac, over a couple of cars to where Leah and Miguel were washing a pickup truck with Melanie and little Amy Robbins. Everyone else had been rotating like crazy, helping out wherever they were needed, but Jenna couldn't help noticing that Leah and Miguel hadn't split up once all day. Sure, Jenna and Peter had mostly worked together too, but that was different. Everyone knew they were just friends.

Jenna dropped her gaze and concentrated on cleaning the wheels of the Cadillac. What Miguel did wasn't her business anymore. No matter what happened, no matter how much it hurt, she'd never, ever tell anyone how disappointed she was that he'd chosen Leah over her. She wished now that she'd never let herself like Miguel in the first place, and she *definitely* wished she hadn't accidentally seen him kissing Leah after the first Eight Prime meeting. In fact, the only good thing about the entire situation was that nobody else knew about her crush on Miguel. Now that the prospect of dating him was hopeless, Jenna could at least take comfort in having had the good sense to keep her feelings to herself.

"All done," Ben announced proudly, waving his towel overhead.

Peter collected five dollars from the driver and tucked the money into his front pocket as the Cadillac drove away.

"Jenna! Jenna, come help us," Jenna's sister Maggie called immediately.

Maggie and Jesse had just started washing a minivan with a troublemaking Junior Explorer named Jason, who'd attached himself to Jesse instantly when he'd learned he was in the presence of a real CCHS Wildcat. Jenna crossed to join them, while Ben and Peter went to work on an old Ford Taurus with Nicole and Courtney.

"Where's Caitlin?" Jenna asked Maggie, dunking her dirty sponge into the nearest bucket before starting in on another set of wheels.

Maggie shrugged. "Who knows? She's been gone forever."

"You're kidding!" Jenna exclaimed. Of all her sisters, Caitlin was by far the shyest. She'd never hung out with anyone but the other Conrad girls, never made any good friends at school. Her best friend had always been her older sister, gregarious Mary Beth. Mary Beth had a million friends and was two years older than Caitlin, so Caitlin was often left alone, but she stayed in Mary Beth's orbit whenever she could, seemingly content on the fringe of the older girl's life. Since Mary Beth had left for college in Nashville, though, Caitlin had become more withdrawn than ever. She had grown *so* timid, in fact, that sometimes Jenna had a hard time believing she had the same genes as the rest of the Conrads.

"I can't believe she just left like that!" Jenna fumed. Caitlin's behavior frustrated her, and frustration made her angry. "Why did she even come if she's so afraid of people?"

"She's coming back," Jesse broke in before Maggie could explain. "She only went to the store to buy us all some sodas."

"Oh." Jenna was mortified that she'd jumped to conclusions, more so because she'd done it in front of Jesse. She could feel her cheeks flushing. "That's a good idea," she added weakly, just as a strong, cold blast of water hit her in the back.

"Gotcha!" Jason screamed triumphantly.

Jenna whirled around into the icy stream long

enough to wrestle the hose out of his hands. Then she turned the water on Jason.

"Hey! No fair!" he squealed, running back and forth in the grass while Jenna kept the hose on him full force. "No fair! Jesse, help me!"

"Sorry, bud," Jesse laughed. "If you're going to mess with the girls, you have to learn to take your lumps."

Peter watched Jenna surreptitiously as he helped Ben, Nicole, and Courtney wash the old Taurus. He'd managed to work next to her most of the day, but he didn't want to be too obvious about it. When Jenna had gone to help Maggie, Peter had decided it was a good idea to go his own way for a change.

"Hey, Peter," said Ben. "What are you doing after the car wash?"

Peter jumped, startled. "Huh? Oh. I'm not sure, but I think I have plans," he answered vaguely.

Ben nodded, clearly disappointed, and Peter made a mental note to invite him to do something sometime. There was no way he was asking Ben to hang out with him tonight, though. Not if things turned out the way he hoped they would.

He glanced over at Jenna again. She had finally let Jason off the hook with the hose, and the two of them were laughing about their battle. Jenna's yellow sweatshirt was soaked and sticking to her, but

Jason looked as if he'd been swimming with his clothes on. Peter watched while Jenna helped the little boy find a clean towel to dry off with, then sent him to join the other Junior Explorers.

Even though he'd known Jenna since sixth grade, lately it seemed like she looked slightly different every time he saw her. No matter how hard Peter tried to memorize her face, the picture wouldn't stay fixed in his mind. He'd think he had it one day at lunchtime; then that same night he'd find himself lying awake, futilely trying to recall a certain feature. Oh, sure, he could always imagine Jenna in a general sort of way. But that wasn't good enough anymore. Peter wanted the details: the sun-streaked strands in her long brown hair, the dimples in her cheeks when she smiled, the four perfect freckles, the tiny, almost completely unnoticeable chip she'd put in one front tooth by falling off his skateboard.

It didn't take a genius to figure out what was going on, and Peter had finally admitted it to himself over the summer.

He was in love.

He didn't even know when it had happened. It wasn't like those love-at-first-sight stories people were always telling, that was for sure. But sometime during the five years he'd been hanging out with Jenna, something had changed. Peter supposed it must have happened at some particular moment—that if a person looked at the whole relationship scientifically, there had to be a dividing line between the days he'd thought of Jenna as a friend and the days he'd spent praying she'd turn into something more. He just had no idea where that line was. Over the summer, though, he'd finally accepted that wherever the line was drawn, he'd crossed a few miles over it—and he'd come to the decision that he had to let Jenna know. It seemed dishonest to pretend everything was the same between them when it wasn't, and Peter believed in honesty.

He also believed in courage, but unfortunately he still hadn't been able to find enough to tell her. Jenna's friendship was the most important thing in the world to him. What if the way he felt now bothered her? What if she didn't want to be his friend anymore after she found out? What if she didn't feel the way he did at all?

What if she never could?

# Two

"Hi! Do you guys need some help?" Melanie asked, walking over to Nicole and Courtney. The girls were stuck by themselves with a big commercial van. "Amy and I are between jobs at the moment," she added, smiling down at her Junior Explorers buddy. "Aren't we, Amy?"

Amy, suddenly shy in front of the two new big girls, clung wide-eyed to Melanie's hand and nodded mutely, her brown curls bobbing down to touch her slender shoulders.

"Yeah. Grab a sponge," Courtney said gratefully. No one had ever officially introduced Melanie to Courtney, but Melanie knew who the other girl was. Everyone at CCHS knew who Melanie was— that part she took for granted.

"No, that's okay," Nicole said hurriedly, contradicting her friend. "We've got it under control."

"You do?" Melanie looked at the enormous white van uncertainly. "Wouldn't it be easier with more people?"

"No," said Nicole.

"Yes!" said Courtney. "Don't be ridiculous, Nicole."

Nicole flinched, and her blue eyes widened angrily. "Courtney!"

"What?"

"Oh . . . never mind!" With a splash, Nicole threw her sponge down into the bucket and stalked off across the parking lot.

"Wow," said Melanie, watching her go. The other girl's back was rigid with emotion and her steps were long and furious. "What's *her* problem?"

Courtney made a face. "I don't think I ought to tell you."

"Why not?"

"Well . . . *you're* kind of her problem." Courtney looked as if she'd like to say more, but then she glanced down at Amy. "I shouldn't have said anything," she mumbled, grabbing the hose and spraying off the side of the van she and Nicole had already washed.

Melanie gave Courtney a long, appraising look. "Amy, sweetie," she said, bending down, "go help the other kids bring in some more cars, okay? I'm going to help Courtney finish this van."

"No, Melanie," Amy whined, tightening her grip on Melanie's fingers. "I want to stay with you. Let me do the bumpers." The little girl strained toward the bucket as if desperate to reach the sponges.

"I promise I'll come get you in a little while, okay? I want to talk to Courtney now."

"No, Melanie. . . ."

"Please, Amy? If we're going to be friends, you have to do what *I* want sometimes."

Amy looked devastated. Tears pooled in her eyes and dampened her thick black lashes. "Do you *promise* you'll come for me soon?"

"Yes." Melanie hugged her little friend tightly. "Now go, okay?"

Amy reluctantly trotted off to join the rest of the Junior Explorers, and Melanie picked up a sponge and started washing next to Courtney. "Okay," she said matter-of-factly. "You want to tell me, so go ahead and spill it."

Courtney looked her over with shrewd green eyes. "I promised Nicole I wouldn't say anything."

"Well, you already did, so you might as well finish what you've started."

"You do know Nicole's my best friend, right? If I tell you, it's only because I want to help her."

"It doesn't look as though she thinks I'll be much help," Melanie observed, nodding in the direction Nicole had stormed off in. She didn't want to say so, but Nicole's behavior had hurt her feelings— and it wasn't the first time, either. People normally liked her, but Nicole had seemed to have it in for her since the very first day they'd met. And Melanie couldn't figure out why.

21

"Look, if I tell you what's going on, will you keep it to yourself?" Courtney asked. "I don't agree with Nicole on this, but she *is* my best friend. . . ."

"What don't you agree with?"

Courtney took a deep breath. "Nicole's convinced that the way Jesse dumped her is all your fault. She thinks if Jesse wasn't so obsessed with you—"

"Wait! Back up!" Melanie interrupted. "Jesse and *Nicole?*"

Courtney's expression was pure surprise. "You didn't know?"

"Know *what?*"

"Oh, wow." Courtney chuckled, shaking her head. "You must have heard what happened at Hank Lundgreen's party?"

Melanie tried to think back to the previous weekend, but with everything else that had happened, it seemed impossibly long ago. "No," she said. "I *didn't* hear."

"You didn't hear that Jesse got totally drunk?"

"So what? That's hardly an event at a football party."

"No. But Jesse was out of control. He made out with Nicole half the night and kept telling her how much he liked her. The sad part is, she believed him. She has a really, really bad crush on the guy."

"Nicole and Jesse *Jones?*" Melanie repeated weakly. The mental picture just wouldn't form.

"Who else? Then on Monday he dumped her hard—told her the whole thing only happened because he'd been drinking. Nicole still can't accept that he'd rather be with you than her."

"He's *not* with me!" Melanie exclaimed. "We're barely even friends."

"That's what I thought!" Courtney cried triumphantly. "I *knew* it wasn't your fault. Now if you could just tell that to Nicole . . ."

Melanie didn't respond as she took a plastic scrub brush to the grill on the front of the van. *Nicole has a problem, all right, but it isn't me*, she thought angrily. The girl had to be at least half responsible for letting Jesse make such a fool of her, and she was insane to blame Melanie for it. It wasn't as if Melanie didn't have enough real problems already without getting involved in Nicole's make-believe ones.

But what irritated Melanie most was that she'd had to hear all this from a virtual stranger . . . that Jesse had hung paintings at her house for hours Wednesday night and never breathed a word about it. *He wouldn't*, she thought, disgusted. *It wouldn't exactly help his futile campaign to impress me*. Still, it was going to be awkward to see Jesse and Nicole at Eight Prime events now. Not only that, but if people already assumed Melanie and Jesse were an item, they probably thought he was cheating on her too. It was embarrassing.

23

"So, are you going to talk to Nicole?" Courtney asked finally, breaking the silence between them.

Melanie shrugged. After what Courtney had just told her, talking to Nicole wasn't anything she was in a hurry to do. She knew for sure now that Nicole didn't like her, and through no fault of her own, either.

"I—" Melanie began.

"Hey! You girls look like you could use some help!" Jesse's booming voice broke in from behind her. "Come on, Ben."

A second later the guys were pitching in on the van. Melanie would have preferred to be rescued by someone else, but at that moment she was glad of any excuse to drop the discussion with Courtney.

The van sparkled at last, and Courtney wandered off to find Nicole while Ben joined Peter and Jenna. Melanie was left alone with Jesse.

"So, how's it going?" he asked. As usual, his smile was confident to the point of being cocky. Nothing could have rubbed her more wrong.

"Fine," she lied, wishing he'd go away.

"Did your dad get back from his business trip?"

"What? Oh, yeah." When Melanie had invited Jesse in on Wednesday, her alcoholic father had been passed out in their poolhouse. She'd told Jesse he was away on business.

"That's too bad," Jesse said, looking her up and

down. "I was thinking I should come over again some night."

"Mmm," Melanie said noncommittally. *Fat chance*, she thought.

"So," Jesse added quickly, "the car wash is going well. I heard Peter say we've washed something like forty cars so far."

"Mmm."

"What's up with you? Are you mad at me or something?"

"Why would I be mad at you?" She'd have loved to say something about his fling with Nicole, but she didn't know what to say.

"I don't know," Jesse replied defensively. "I haven't done anything."

She stared at him coolly.

"Aw, is it the paintings? You got in trouble for hanging those stupid paintings, didn't you? I *told* you your dad would be mad."

Melanie bristled. Those "stupid paintings," as Jesse called them, had been painted by her mother, who had died in a car wreck two years before.

"It isn't the paintings," Melanie managed to say without shouting. Far from being angry, her father had cried when he'd seen them again. They were all exactly where Melanie and Jesse had hung them—all except Mrs. Andrews's self-portrait. Her dad apparently still found that one too painful to look at. He'd slipped it back into the storage room while Melanie was at school.

"What, then?" Jesse demanded.

"Nothing. I have to go."

"Melanie!"

But she was already hurrying across the park, putting distance between them as quickly as she could. She'd been an idiot to let a guy like Jesse get even as close as he had. It wouldn't happen again.

The Junior Explorers were still filing up and down the edge of Clearwater Boulevard. Melanie headed toward them, noticing that their signs were dragging on the grass behind them now instead of being waved jubilantly overhead. The poor kids looked as exhausted as Melanie suddenly felt.

"Melanie!" Amy cried excitedly when she saw her. "You came back!"

"I said I would," Melanie murmured, catching the small girl as she flung herself into her arms.

"Big people always say things they don't mean."

"Well . . ." Melanie couldn't argue with that. "I don't."

She took Amy's hand and straightened up, planning to head back to the pavement to wash more cars. As she raised her eyes, though, she spotted Tiffany Barrett driving down the street in a black sedan.

"Tiff!" Melanie called out, waving to her fellow cheerleader. "Tiffany!"

The car slowed abruptly. Tiffany had seen her and was checking out the scene in the park. Melanie watched as Tiffany took in the tired-looking Junior Explorers, the handmade car wash signs, and the chaos in the parking lot. Her glossy red lips curled into a condescending smirk, and then, with a nod toward Melanie, Tiffany drove on by.

"Oh, I *hate* that girl!" Melanie exclaimed without thinking. Even if Tiffany didn't want her car washed, she could at least have stopped to say hello. And that superior look on her face!

"It's not nice to hate people," Amy said placidly. "That's what they told us in Sunday school."

"Well—I—uh . . . you're right," Melanie stammered, taken by surprise. "I didn't really mean that."

Amy smiled, and Melanie knew her crime was forgiven. "Is she mean?" the little girl asked conspiratorially. "You can tell me."

"Yeah," Melanie answered, amused. "She's *real* mean."

"Mean people suck."

"Amy! I'll bet they didn't teach you *that* in Sunday school!"

"No. That's what my daddy says."

"Well, I'm not sure he meant for you to repeat it."

But Melanie couldn't help laughing to herself as she walked her little friend back to the car wash.

Amy's daddy had a definite point.

"What's the final count, Nicole?" Peter asked, eager to learn how successful the car wash had been. "How did we do?"

"We made three hundred and fifteen dollars," Nicole answered, putting the last stack of bills back into the rusted cash box.

"That's not very good!" Jenna said, her voice full of disappointment.

"It's sixty-three cars," Leah pointed out. "I think that's pretty good."

"It felt more like a hundred and sixty-three," Jenna grumbled. "I'm exhausted." There were snickers around the group, but Jenna didn't smile.

"Leah's right, Jenna," said Peter, trying to cheer her up. "It's a lot more money than we had this morning."

"Sure," Ben agreed. "We knew this wasn't going to happen overnight." The happy way he said it made Peter suspect that Ben wouldn't mind if earning the Junior Explorers a bus took every weekend between then and graduation.

"We just have to have a little faith," Peter said, winking at Jenna. She smiled reluctantly in return. "Pass the cash box, Nicole!" he commanded happily.

Nicole passed the box to Courtney, who passed it to Leah, who passed it to Jenna, and so on around the circle of eleven: Eight Prime plus Courtney Bell and the Conrad sisters. Chris and Maura had already gone home, along with the Junior Explorers, and dusk was falling in the park. The huge oak and sycamore trees at the edges of the parking lot cast shadows that blanketed the grass and crept out onto the still-wet asphalt.

The cash box finished its circuit, ending in Peter's hands. "Well, I guess that's all for tonight," he said. "I'll put this into our bank account."

"When are we meeting again?" asked Melanie. The group looked at Peter expectantly.

"Thursday night? My house?"

Everyone agreed before they broke up and drifted off in ones and twos, picking up the scattered car washing equipment as they went. Nicole took the card table but left the cash box with Peter. Soon he and the Conrad girls were the only people still in the lot.

"I'm starving," said Maggie. "Let's go."

"Are you ready, Jenna?" Caitlin asked. She had driven the three of them in their mother's car.

"I guess so," said Jenna. "I'll see you at church tomorrow, Peter."

"All right." Peter watched, feeling as deflated as last summer's inner tube, as the girls started off across the parking lot. He'd been planning to ask Jenna to do something with him after the car wash, but he'd never gotten the chance. They hadn't been alone together for even a single minute.

*I should have asked her anyway,* he berated himself as Jenna's figure faded into the growing darkness. *No one would have thought anything of it.* He sighed gloomily. *Not even Jenna.*

"Jenna! Hey, Jenna!" he called impulsively, running after her. He caught up halfway across the parking lot. "I just decided to go out for pizza. Want to come?" He felt rude asking her in front of Maggie and Caitlin without inviting them, but it was the best excuse he could think of so late in the game.

"Sure," Jenna said, smiling. "That sounds great."

The two of them waved good-bye to Caitlin and Maggie, then climbed into Peter's old metallic blue Toyota. The Tercel was really the Altmann family's third car, but since Peter's only sibling, David, was away at college, Peter drove it most of the time.

"So where do you want to go?" Peter asked. He was trying his best to sound casual, but even he could hear the too-excited edge in his voice.

"Slice of Rome, don't you think?" Jenna replied, apparently not noticing. "They make the best pizza. Besides, we're not exactly dressed for anything fancier." She glanced down at her dirt-spattered jeans and still-damp sweatshirt, then over at his equally soggy clothes. Peter would have liked to take her somewhere nicer, but he saw her point.

"Yeah. Slice of Rome is good." He turned the car in that direction. With everything else on his mind, though, they were nearly to the restaurant before he realized they'd been driving in total silence. "You're quiet tonight," he ventured.

"I'm tired. We have to do something less exhausting for our next fund-raiser."

"That would be okay with me. Do you have any ideas?"

"Not yet, but I will. Maybe we ought to sell something."

Peter nodded thoughtfully as he pulled the Tercel into the crowded restaurant parking lot. "That could work."

Slice of Rome was packed wall-to-wall with the Saturday-night dinner crowd. Peter and Jenna ended up at a tiny table for two at the very back of the restaurant. "I'm sorry, but this is all we have," the teenage hostess apologized. "Unless you want to wait."

"No, this is fine," Peter assured her. It certainly wasn't the romantic venue of his imagination, but considering how crowded the place was, they could have done a lot worse. He and Jenna wriggled into their tight seats and ordered the house special with a pitcher of root beer.

"You seemed pretty disappointed we didn't make more money at the car wash," Peter said while they waited for the food.

Jenna shrugged. "I was, a little. I mean, we

worked really *hard*. . . . We had all those extra people helping us. And we didn't even come close to what just eight of us made at Kurt's carnival booth."

"True. But the money we made today was straight profit, whereas at the carnival they still had to pay for the food and plates and everything out of that thousand dollars we took in. Not only that, but the carnival had a built-in crowd to sell to. Today we had to bring in our own customers."

"You're right," Jenna said, but she didn't sound too convinced. "When you put it like that, I guess we did okay."

"We did! And next time we'll do even better."

"Uh-huh." Jenna was staring off into space across the noisy restaurant, absently twirling a strand of hair around her index finger.

"Are you all right?" Peter asked.

"Fine." Her finger kept twirling.

"You seem kind of distracted."

"What? Oh." Jenna turned her gaze back to him and smiled apologetically, making dimples in her cheeks. "I'm sorry. I don't know why I'm so tired. I probably should have gone straight home."

"You'll feel better once you have something to eat."

"Maybe," Jenna agreed. But a dullness in her blue eyes said she doubted it. Peter hadn't even begun to make his move and he was already getting cold feet. The way Jenna was acting was just plain strange.

The waitress brought their drinks. Peter poured them both a root beer from the pitcher, then stabbed at the ice in his glass with a straw. He had intended to talk to Jenna tonight. He had *hoped* to work his way around to the secret that was driving him crazy. But Jenna didn't seem like herself at all, and the pressure of trying to put his feelings into words was crushing enough without catching his friend in a rare bad mood. Peter was at a loss.

*I have no idea what to say to her,* he realized. *Not to mention no idea exactly when to say it.*

Now didn't seem like a good time, though. The longer Jenna sat there with that blank look on her face, the more nervous Peter became.

At last the pizza arrived. Jenna reached for a slice immediately. "Hooray," she said, sliding it backward onto her plate, trailing strings of gooey cheese across the table. "I was afraid I'd fall asleep before it got here."

"It looks good, though," Peter said, helping himself.

Jenna nodded absently, already lost in space again.

*No. Tonight definitely isn't the night for major revelations,* Peter thought, chickening out. He'd waited this long. He could wait a little longer.

# Three

Melanie walked through the cafeteria at lunchtime on Monday, her unappetizing-looking tray held stiffly out in front of her. *I really have to start making my lunch at home,* she thought as she slid into a seat at the table with the rest of the cheerleaders.

"Mmm. Fish sticks," Tanya Jeffries teased, rubbing her bare brown midriff as if they looked delicious. Tanya's home-packed lunch was spread out on the table in front of her—her peanut butter sandwich, carrot sticks, and apple seemed like a gourmet feast compared to the slop on Melanie's tray.

"I know," Melanie replied disgustedly. "I'm already about to gag, so cut me some slack, okay?"

Tanya grinned. "Get enough ketchup on those and you won't be able to taste anything else."

"That's the plan." Melanie picked up the ketchup and began burying her lunch in a sea of red.

"Hey, Melanie," Tiffany said. "I saw you in the park this weekend."

"Yeah, I saw you too. Nice stop."

Tiffany laughed as if amazed. "You didn't really expect me to stop in the middle of that mess, did you? With all those little kids? What were you doing, anyway?"

"I thought it was pretty obvious we were having a car wash."

"You're right. As soaked and filthy as you all were, that part *was* obvious. What I really meant was *why?*"

Melanie took a deep breath before she answered. As the only sophomore on the cheering squad, she always felt like she needed to watch her words with the other girls. Except for Tiffany—with Tiffany she needed to watch her back.

"If you need to know, a few of us are trying to earn enough money to buy a bus for a program for underprivileged children. We're going to give it to the kids in Kurt Englbehrt's memory. That's what the car wash was for."

"You couldn't find a more dignified way to honor Kurt's memory?" Tiffany asked, horrified.

"I think it's nice," Angela Maldonado cut in quickly. "You should have asked me, Melanie. I'd have helped you."

"Me too," said Tanya.

Lou Anne, Vanessa, and Sue stared uncomfortably at the ceiling, but Cindy seemed somewhat interested.

"I'll keep it in mind," Melanie promised, noting all their attitudes. "It's probably going to take us a year to earn enough money, so we'll need help again sometime."

"There goes your social life," Tiffany drawled delightedly. "No more parties for you!"

Tiffany's comment gave Melanie a thought. "Speaking of parties," she said, ignoring the part about her social life, "didn't you all go to that one at Hank Lundgreen's last week?"

Several heads nodded.

"Why didn't anyone tell me Jesse Jones spent the night making out with Nicole Brewster?" It wasn't as if Melanie expected a full written report or anything, but still . . . the way the cheerleaders loved to gossip, it seemed strange no one had even *mentioned* it.

"Was that her name?" Vanessa asked in a bored tone.

"You know who she is, Vanessa. She tried out for cheerleader last year," Melanie replied, annoyed.

"So did something like eighty-six other girls. You don't expect me to remember the name of every loser who comes out for the squad, do you?" She and Melanie locked eyes.

"We *wanted* to tell you, Melanie," Angela put in. "But we didn't want to hurt your feelings."

"That's the truth," Lou Anne added. "We knew

you'd be upset that Jesse was cheating on you. Besides, he dumped her the next day."

Melanie sat speechless. It was even worse than she had feared. If the *cheerleaders* thought she and Jesse were together, probably so did the rest of the school. *Not only that, but if I did like Jesse, not telling me would be the worst thing they could do.* She looked around the table at her so-called friends, then took a long, deep breath.

"I'm going to say this one time, so listen up," she told them, struggling to keep her voice calm. "I'd rather shave my head and become a nun than ever date Jesse Jones. There is absolutely *nothing* between us. Got it?"

"Anyway, that's over now," said Vanessa, brushing it aside.

Melanie's temper flared at her squad leader's condescending attitude, but she nodded mutely. It *was* over. She tried to push the distracting image of Jesse and Nicole from her mind.

"And since we're all together," Vanessa continued, "I think we ought to talk about the game against Cave Creek next week. I have a new stunt in mind, and I want us to start working up to it this afternoon."

"This afternoon!" Cindy protested. "We don't have practice on Monday!"

"We do now," said Vanessa. "I'm calling extra practices for the next two weeks. I want to get this stunt ready in time for the game. We'll meet every day if we have to."

Tiffany groaned, and for once Melanie agreed with her. When Melanie had tried out for the squad, she'd thought being a cheerleader was going to be great. Now her feelings were mixed. Cheering was a lot of fun, but all the politics and backbiting and kissing up to Vanessa were getting on her nerves.

In theory, the girls had a faculty advisor, but Ms. Carson was overloaded with French, Italian, and Latin classes and didn't know anything about cheerleading anyway. She sat in the stands during games and dropped in on an occasional practice, but that was about it. The reality of the situation was that Vanessa called the shots, simply telling Ms. Carson what they were doing from time to time.

"You've got a problem with that, Barrett?" Vanessa asked, looking sideways at Tiffany.

"Excuse me for having a life," Tiffany retorted. She was a senior and therefore less cowed by Vanessa's bullying.

Vanessa's eyes narrowed. "Well, get rid of it. If you miss a practice, you're off the squad."

Tiffany rolled her eyes but bit back her reply.

"Good. I'll see you all in the gym at three, then," Vanessa said, right as the end-of-lunch bell rang.

The cheerleaders rose hurriedly to their feet, and Melanie wondered if everyone was as eager to get out of there as she was. She was almost to the exit when Jesse snuck up behind her.

"Guess who?" he flirted, slipping rough hands over her eyes. His fingers smelled of fish sticks and ketchup.

"Let go of me, Jesse," she warned. Now that the cheerleaders had confirmed Courtney's story about his fooling around with Nicole, Melanie was even more disgusted with him than before.

"What's the deal?" Jesse demanded, taking his hands away. "Why are you in such a bad mood?"

"Maybe I don't appreciate being grabbed," she said angrily. "Why don't you think about what you're doing? For once."

"Huh?" Jesse's expression was baffled.

Melanie hesitated a second, on the verge of telling him off, then changed her mind. Why waste her breath? He'd never change. With an exasperated toss of her head, she turned and walked out of the cafeteria.

"Do you want to come in?" Leah asked.

Miguel had driven up to the front of the condominium building where the Rosenthals lived, and now the two of them sat in his car at the curb.

"My parents aren't home, but I don't think they'd mind," she added.

"Are you sure?" Miguel glanced uncertainly at the modern four-story structure. "My mom would have a heart attack if she came home and found my sister Rosa alone with some strange guy."

Leah laughed. "Are you strange? Maybe I should pay more attention."

"You know what I mean," said Miguel. "I'm strange to your parents."

"Well, they did find your interest in water polo a little inexplicable."

"Water polo!" he cried, offended. "What's wrong with water polo?"

"Nothing," she said, laughing at his outraged expression. "I'm kidding."

"You told them I play water polo, though?"

"Well . . . yeah. I think I mentioned it."

"What else did you tell them about me?" he asked.

Leah shrugged. "Just that you're on the water polo team and in my biology class. And that we worked together at Kurt's carnival, and now we're both in Eight Prime. That's about all, I think."

"Did you tell them about my dad and . . . everything?"

"Of course not! I told you I can keep a secret."

Relief flooded his dark eyes.

"So what have you told your mom about me?" Leah asked curiously.

"Well . . . nothing yet." Miguel seemed suddenly uneasy as he fiddled with the gear shift.

"*Nothing?*"

40

"Not yet."

"Miguel! You haven't even mentioned me?"

"If I do, she'll just want to meet you. You know how mothers are."

"What's wrong with that? I *want* you to meet *my* parents."

"And I want you to meet my mother," Miguel assured her. "It's not like I'm keeping you a *secret* or anything. It just hasn't come up yet. I mean, after all, it hasn't even been a week since . . . you know."

Leah smiled, remembering the day they'd gotten together at the lake. "Have you told *anyone* about me?" she asked, scooting to the edge of her seat and snuggling into his shoulder.

Miguel put his arm around her and pulled her closer. "Who would I tell? Besides, I like it this way, don't you? Just between the two of us?"

"For now."

The fact was, there wasn't anyone Leah really wanted to tell either. If her best friend, Daryl, hadn't moved away, she'd have probably felt differently, but Daryl was gone. Besides, once word got out at school that Miguel del Rios was seeing someone, it would draw the curious like a car wreck. Leah could imagine the gossip: *He's seeing* who? *Leah* who? *What's he doing with* her?

It *was* better keeping their relationship a secret. For now.

———

"I'm home!" Jenna announced, slamming the front door.

"How was school, dear?" Mrs. Conrad asked, wandering out from the kitchen with a recipe card in one hand and a mildly harried expression on her face.

"Fine," said Jenna, hoping God would forgive the white lie. School had stunk like never before. "I've got a lot of homework, though."

Mrs. Conrad ran a distracted hand through her graying auburn hair. "You'd better get to it, then. I'm making meat loaf and mashed potatoes for dinner." Jenna wasn't sure how those two thoughts were related, unless her mother was trying to give her something to look forward to. Mrs. Conrad's meat loaf was a church potluck legend.

"Okay, sounds good," Jenna said over her shoulder as she climbed the stairs to the room she shared with Maggie. Jenna loved her mother, and on another day she might have followed her into the kitchen and poured her heart out. But right then Jenna wasn't in the mood to talk to anyone—not after just seeing Leah and Miguel drive off in his car together after school.

It was getting harder and harder to pretend she didn't know what was going on between those two, and more difficult still to act like she didn't care. After all, she'd been dreaming about Miguel for two whole years, and she'd been excited about her new friendship with Leah, too. In a lot of ways, it would have been easier to accept if Miguel had picked a stranger. But *Leah* . . . and he hadn't even known her that long! It wasn't fair.

Then Jenna opened her bedroom door and almost lost her cool completely. Maggie's side of the room was a disaster. Discarded clothes lay in rumpled heaps on Maggie's blue comforter and spilled over onto the hardwood floor. Her backpack looked as if it had exploded, spewing its contents from her tiny desktop onto her bed, the floor, and the dresser. But the coup de grâce was the pale pink bra and panties her little sister had peeled off and left right in the middle of the floor.

"Maggie!" Jenna shouted.

"Maggie is swimming at the Y with Becky Leary," her mother called from downstairs.

Jenna hesitated in her doorway, trying to decide what, if anything, to say to her mother about the condition of her room. "Okay," she yelled back finally, her voice half strangled with barely suppressed anger.

There was no point involving her mom. Jenna had complained to her parents a hundred times about having to share a room with Maggie, but no one ever did anything to fix it. *It's the perfect ending to the perfect day, really*, she thought bitterly, walking into her room and slamming the door behind her. She threw herself down on her bed and glared across the small strip of floor that divided her side of the room from Maggie's.

*When Caitlin was a junior, Mary Beth moved out and Caitlin had a private room for her last two years of high school,* Jenna thought, redirecting her poisonous stare from her little sister's mess to the ceiling, above which lay her older sister's attic bedroom. *She still has her own room!* Caitlin's was the only room on the third floor—no one else even went up there. *Forget about her own room, she has her own floor!*

It was so unfair . . . so frustrating. Why couldn't Caitlin get a job or go to college and move out like any normal eighteen-year-old? But whenever Jenna dared to ask that perfectly reasonable question, her parents looked at her as if she were the biggest traitor in the history of families.

Jenna sat up, only to come face-to-face with Maggie's underwear again.

"That's really the limit," she said aloud. "If I can't get rid of Caitlin, at least I can teach Maggie some manners."

Sliding to her feet, Jenna picked up the offending articles of lingerie and looked around the room for something suitably educational to do with them. She knew Maggie had gotten the set as part of her fall school wardrobe—the new eighth-grader had been thrilled about how pretty and grown-up the bra was when she'd brought it home. But here it

44

was, only three weeks later, and the scrap of lacy pink satin had already been discarded on the floor, along with the matching panties.

A late-afternoon breeze gusted through the open window just then, billowing the yellow gingham curtains. Jenna felt the cool wind on her cheek, and an inspired grin spread slowly across her face.

The wide wooden sill along the bottom of the window jutted into Jenna's bedroom on the inside of the house and into second-story space on the outside. Jenna crossed the room hurriedly and glanced down into the Conrads' large, grassy backyard. No one was around. Her smile grew even broader.

Sticking her head through the opening, Jenna checked the windowsill. Sure enough, there were four big rusted nails still sticking out of it from the string of Christmas lights she and Maggie had put there in December. With intense satisfaction, Jenna hung Maggie's bra from the nail at one end of the sill and her underpants from the nail at the other. They were invisible from inside the bedroom, but anyone standing in the backyard would see them clearly, flapping in the breeze.

Maggie would be mortified.

*It serves her right*, Jenna thought, half tempted to telephone Maggie's big crush, Scott Jenner, and invite him over for a cookout. Maybe she'd even put up a sign: MAGGIE'S DIRTY UNDERWEAR. That would teach her!

*And me,* Jenna thought with a wince, imagining what her parents would do if they caught her hanging Maggie's unmentionables out the window.

*Do unto others, Jenna,* she could practically hear her mother saying. *Treat other people the way you want to be treated.* It was one of the most basic rules of Christianity, but it was also one of the hardest. Especially at times like this, when everything in her life was going so wrong. Besides, didn't Maggie deserve a little grief?

*Turn the other cheek. Forgive and you will be forgiven.* The phrases had been drilled into her head so many times that they were right there for her now, right on the tip of her tongue. Jenna hesitated, looking down at the funny pink flags flying from her windowsill.

*Maybe I shouldn't do this after all. Maybe I should bring Maggie's stuff back inside and put it in the hamper like a nice sister.*

*Yeah, and maybe Maggie should kiss my foot,* retorted an angry, fed-up voice in her head. *It's not like I'm turning her out in a snowstorm without a coat or anything. It's only a silly prank.* The smile crept back onto Jenna's face. A silly prank that for some reason made her feel a whole lot better.

"Done, then," she decided, leaving the window. "Done, and no turning back!"

But even with that little bit of revenge to console her, Jenna still couldn't bear the sight of her sister's mess in their small room. *I'll go downstairs and work on the computer*, she decided, grabbing her backpack off her bed and walking out onto the landing.

The Conrads shared one computer, and it was downstairs in the den. *I can log on to the CCHS Web site and see if Mrs. Wilson's posted the answers for the geometry homework we turned in this morning. That way I'll know if I'm on the right track before I start today's problems.*

Jenna trotted down the stairs, happy with her plan. *Or I could call Miguel and ask him what answers he got. . . .*

*No. Bad idea.* She wouldn't even know what to say to him. Besides, he was probably still hanging out with Leah. The mere thought sucked anything resembling enthusiasm right out of Jenna's step.

Of all the girls at school, why did he have to choose Leah?

# Four

"You'd never know it was supposed to be fall with the weather still this hot," Jenna grumbled as she and Peter walked across the student parking lot after school on Tuesday.

Peter shrugged. "It's not *that* hot." It was warm for so late in September, but the sky was clear and a light breeze blew. "I think it's pretty nice."

Jenna looked at him as if he were out of his mind. "It's hot!"

"Well . . . if it's so hot, I guess we'd better stop for ice cream."

Jenna grimaced, then smiled. "You knew that's what I wanted all along, didn't you?"

"I try to stay on top of things." Peter chuckled quietly to himself as he opened Jenna's door, then walked around behind the old Toyota and climbed in on the driver's side.

"So where should we go?" Jenna asked.

Peter buckled his seat belt. "We could head over to McKinney's," he said, naming a popular mom-and-pop shop a couple of blocks from the school.

"We could, but it will probably be dinnertime before we see any ice cream. I'll bet the line's out the door already."

"Where do you want to go, then? I get the feeling you've got someplace in mind."

"How about that place over by the park? It ought to be a lot less crowded than it is on the weekends."

"Okay." Peter started the engine and pulled out onto the street, headed downtown.

Jenna's idea turned out to be a good one—the cute, old-fashioned ice cream parlor was practically deserted. They ordered hot fudge sundaes, then sat down together at a white wrought-iron table for two.

"Now, this is more like it," Jenna said, waving her long silver spoon in the air before plunging it into her sundae. It sank swiftly through the layers of nuts, whipped cream, and hot fudge, finally encountering resistance in two enormous scoops of vanilla ice cream. "Mmm." She scooped out a big gooey bite with a huge smile.

Peter smiled too as he dug into his own identical sundae. He'd never met anyone with as big a sweet tooth as Jenna. Just seeing her grin that way made the trip downtown completely worthwhile.

"Good, huh?" Jenna asked.

"Yeah."

But in truth Peter barely tasted the ice cream he was eating. Ever since he'd lost his nerve at the pizza place Saturday night, he'd been thinking about what he'd say to Jenna the first time he got a chance like this one. Unfortunately, his big come-clean speech still hadn't progressed much beyond *Jenna, I've been thinking. . . .* He knew he had to say *something.* It wasn't right to let things go on as if nothing had changed. Not even if that course of action was looking smarter every day.

*After all, how do I know I'm really in love with her?* he asked himself. *I love Jenna, sure—she's my best friend. But that's not the same as being* in love *with her. If I'm wrong, I could ruin everything.*

But Peter didn't think he was wrong.

*No, I have to tell her,* he thought. *It's the only honest thing to do.* As Jenna finished her sundae, he racked his brain for a natural-sounding way to broach the subject.

"Perfect!" Jenna declared, dropping her spoon into her empty sundae glass. "That was just what I needed." She did look less flushed, but that was as likely to be due to the air conditioning as the ice cream. Then she suddenly seemed to notice that Peter had stopped eating.

"What's the matter? Don't you feel well?" The worry in her eyes showed how little she comprehended a lack of interest in hot fudge.

"No, I'm fine." Peter took a deep breath. "Jenna, do you ever think about us?"

"Huh? Of course. . . . What about us?"

"Well, uh, you know," Peter said. "Our friendship and stuff."

Jenna looked puzzled. "What kind of stuff?"

"Like, well . . . do you think we'll still be friends after we graduate?"

"Of course. Why wouldn't we be?"

"I don't know." Peter nervously stirred the melted remains of his sundae.

"Is something the matter?" she asked, leaning forward across the small table. "Is this about college?"

"College?" he repeated, startled.

"You still want to go to College of the Ozarks, right? You aren't backing out on me."

"What? Oh. No, of course not." Peter and Jenna had decided to attend the small Protestant college together all the way back in eighth grade. Most of their other friends, even the Christian ones, thought they were crazy to consider such a tiny, rural school, but so far neither one had wavered. Huge Clearwater University was a distant second choice in comparison.

"Whew!" Jenna settled back into her seat. "If you bailed out on me after all this time, I don't know if I could forgive you."

Peter smiled a little. "You'd have to. The Bible says so."

"Hmm. Well, okay. But does it say I have to *like* you after that?" The dimples in her cheeks twitched

51

mischievously, as if ever not liking him was the biggest impossibility she could imagine.

And that was when Peter knew he couldn't tell her how he felt. Not then, anyway. Not there. He couldn't take a chance on saying the wrong thing. Not to be friends with Jenna anymore, not to go to college with her, was about the worst thing he could imagine.

*It's not worth it*, he thought, giving up. *There's just too much to lose.*

"Oh, wait. I want to go in here." Courtney made a quick turn inside the crowded indoor mall and beelined for a store called U.S. Girls.

"So do I," said Nicole, hurrying after her friend. "Look at that cute pair of jeans," she added, pointing to a mannequin in the window. She was a few steps closer when she saw a poster hanging like a banner inside the entrance to the store.

ARE YOU A U.S. GIRL? it asked in red-white-and-blue-striped letters. WE WANT YOU!

Nicole quickly scanned the rest of the short text, her heart beating faster with every word she read. The chain of U.S. Girls clothing stores was having a modeling contest—and anyone could enter!

"Courtney, look!" she breathed, her eyes glued to the poster.

" 'Are you a U.S. Girl?' " Courtney read in a sarcastic tone of voice. "Yadda, yadda, yadda . . ." Her eyes scanned down the lines. " 'Help us launch our new line of U.S. Girls jeans by participating in our nationwide model search. Missouri hopefuls compete in St. Louis. Details inside.' So? What about it?"

"Wouldn't it be fun to enter?" Nicole could almost see herself walking a runway in U.S. Girls jeans, a rolled red bandanna tied in her blond hair.

"You're not serious!" Courtney scoffed. "No offense, Nicole, but that's a national contest. Besides, I've got a big picture of your parents letting you drive all the way to St. Louis to compete. Do yourself a favor and forget it."

"Uh-huh," Nicole answered vaguely, nodding. But she knew she wouldn't forget it for a minute until the contest was held. As soon as Courtney wandered off to look at a display of fall sweaters, Nicole sidled up to the sales counter, where entry blanks for the modeling contest were set out in a patriotic-looking cardboard holder next to the register. She took one quickly, folding it up and stuffing it into her back pocket before Courtney could catch her.

"What do you think of this?" Courtney called. Nicole spun around to see her friend holding an apple green angora sweater up to her neck, smoothing it over her well-endowed chest.

"Is that your color?" Nicole asked uncertainly, secretly wondering if Courtney had seen her take the entry blank.

Courtney smiled and her green eyes gleamed. "If a redhead can't wear it, who can? I'm going to try it on." She walked off in the direction of the dressing rooms, and Nicole seized the opportunity to check out the new U.S. Girls jeans.

There were only three styles, and Nicole knew right away which ones would be best for the contest: the seventies retro pair with the visible buttons up the front and the small cinching buckle in the back to keep them nice and tight. Jeans like that would show every excess ounce a girl had on her.

*But you wouldn't have any excess ounces*, Nicole thought as she grabbed a couple of sizes off the rack and headed toward the dressing rooms. She peeked under the doors of the dressing stalls until she found Courtney's feet, then shut herself into the booth beside her friend's. "How's the sweater?" she asked through the partition.

"Jeff is going to like it," Courtney answered with obvious satisfaction. "It's right up his alley."

"I didn't think you'd been dating the guy long enough to know what was up his alley," Nicole returned, trying to keep the bitterness out of her voice. She wanted to be happy for Court, but it was hard not to be jealous. Especially since Courtney had met Jeff at the same party where Jesse had kissed Nicole—and things had turned out so differently for the two of them. Jesse had dropped Nicole like a bad habit. Meanwhile, Courtney and Jeff had already been out on two dates, with a third one scheduled for that weekend. Why couldn't *Jeff* have turned out to be the jerk?

"Skintight is up every guy's alley," Courtney declared confidently. "What are you trying on?"

"Jeans." Nicole slipped hurriedly out of the skirt she'd been wearing and began pulling on a pair in her regular size.

"U.S. Girls jeans?" Courtney asked, clearly amused. Her dressing room door slammed as she let herself out.

"So what? They're cute," Nicole defended herself. They were *very* cute, in fact, and Nicole was thrilled to discover that her usual size was too big on her. The pants gapped at the waist and sagged in the seat. Nicole gazed into the three-way mirror until her smile became enormous. All that dieting was really paying off.

"You're not still thinking about that stupid contest, I hope," Courtney said, hovering outside Nicole's dressing room.

"No," Nicole lied quickly. "I just need some jeans."

"Yeah, sure you do. Well, I'll be waiting outside whenever you get through fantasizing."

Nicole listened as Courtney's footsteps faded away. Then she shimmied out of the jeans and reached for a smaller pair. Whereas the first ones had been too large, these were almost too tight.

Nicole struggled to fasten the final button and turned to scrutinize herself from the side. Her stomach was flatter than it had ever been in her life, and she had been right about the style showing off thinness to advantage. Sucking in her abdomen, Nicole tried to imagine what she'd look like in the next size smaller still. The contest was four weeks away—if she decided to enter, she had plenty of time to step up her diet.

*If* she decided to enter? No. She *had* to enter. The longer she looked in the mirror, the more certain she became.

Nicole understood that in a contest open to girls from fifty states the odds weren't in her favor. She also knew that getting her parents to let her drive more than a hundred miles to St. Louis was going to take some major begging. But she couldn't help thinking that Courtney was missing an important point: in clothes modeling, it was more important to be thin than beautiful.

And Nicole was getting very, very thin.

When Jenna got home from eating ice cream with Peter, Maggie was pacing their room in a frenzy, bouncing back and forth like a Ping-Pong ball at the Chinese Nationals.

"Have you seen my new bra?" she demanded the second Jenna stepped through the door.

"What? Oh." A sly smile curled Jenna's lips. "Which bra?" she asked innocently.

"The pink one!" Maggie replied, half frantic. "The one I just got when school started."

"The one with the matching underpants?"

"Yes!"

"Oh."

"Well? Have you seen it?"

"Not lately." Jenna had come in through the front door, so that wasn't a lie. She hadn't seen her sister's missing lingerie since she'd hung it out the window the afternoon before.

"I've looked everywhere!" Maggie wailed. "I don't know where it could be!" She threw herself down on her bed, frustrated almost to the point of tears.

Jenna noticed that her sister's side of the room had been cleared of dirty clothes. Not only that, but it looked as if the stuff on Maggie's desk had been straightened up too. Jenna sat down on the edge of her own bed, thoroughly enjoying the sight of her sister in such a tizzy.

"Have you looked under your bed?" she asked.

"Yes."

"And in your dresser drawers?"

"Of course."

"How about the laundry room?"

"Yes. Yes, yes, yes!" Maggie fell face forward into her pillow, her corkscrew curls cascading over the coverlet and hiding her freckled face. "It's gone! I—I must have left it in the locker room after gym, and someone took it."

"Do you honestly believe you could have gotten dressed without underwear and not noticed?"

"No. Yes . . . I don't know." She lifted her head just long enough to shoot Jenna a tragic look before she dropped it back to her pillow. "That was my *favorite* bra," she said in a muffled voice.

"Oh. Then have you looked out the window?"

Maggie's head jerked up like a marionette's. "Say what?"

It took every bit of self-control Jenna had not to laugh out loud. "I *said*, have you looked out the window?"

Maggie stared at Jenna as if Jenna had gone insane. "Of course not."

Jenna shrugged, then lay back on her bed and laced her fingers behind her head, savoring the moment. It didn't last long. Slowly, suspiciously, Maggie turned her gaze toward the open window, where the lightweight gingham curtains were blowing in the breeze.

"Why would my bra be out the window?" she asked, her eyes narrowing to slits. She got to her feet and stood glaring down at Jenna, still stretched out on her bed. "Jenna?"

It was too much. After one last attempt to keep a straight face, Jenna burst out laughing.

Maggie rushed to the window. "I don't see any . . . ," she began, looking out toward the yard. Then she happened to glance down.

"*Oh!*" Maggie snatched up the articles hanging from the windowsill and spun around with a slip of pink satin in each trembling hand. "How *could* you?" she demanded, outraged.

"How could *you* leave your disgusting filthy underwear in the middle of the floor?" Jenna countered. "You're not the only person who has to live in this room, you know."

"But someone could have *seen* them!" Maggie cried, her voice rising to a screech. "I can't believe you *did* that!"

"Oh, relax," Jenna told her, still laughing. "No one saw them unless they were standing in our backyard." She tapped her chin thoughtfully. "Although, come to think of it, I did notice Scott Jenner and a few of his buddies out biking around the neighborhood yesterday. I suppose . . . if you got the angle from the sidewalk just right . . ."

Maggie looked as if she might pass out. "You'd better be lying, Jenna," she warned.

"Maybe I am, maybe I'm not."

Maggie glared furiously, only shifting her gaze to inspect her lingerie for damage. "You know, it could have rained, Jenna," she said angrily, checking the delicate fabric. "Or they could have blown down. Or gotten ripped. You're lucky they're not ruined."

"No. *You're* lucky," Jenna corrected, finally getting serious. "If you leave them on the floor again, things might not go as well."

"What's that supposed to mean?" Maggie asked, her hands on her hips.

"It means I'm tired of living with a pig! You'd better shape up, Maggie, and that's the truth. I'm not putting up with your messes anymore."

"You—you—this is my room too!" Maggie sputtered furiously. "I'll get you back, Jenna!"

Jenna rolled her eyes. "Oooh, I'm so scared," she said, trembling with feigned fear.

Maggie glared a moment longer, then threw her bra and underwear down onto the floor and ran out of the room.

"Eighth-graders!" Jenna muttered.

Then she smiled. The pale pink sources of yesterday's irritation were so far on Maggie's side of the room, they were practically hugging the wall. Her sister clearly wasn't taking any chances.

"Well, what do you know?" Jenna said with a giggle. "You *can* teach an old pig new tricks."

# Five

Melanie was walking to her last class on Wednesday when Jesse ran up to catch her in the hallway. He reached for her elbow, then apparently thought better of it, dropping his hand before he touched her. Melanie smiled slightly. Apparently she'd finally made her point, but she still wasn't in any mood to forgive him. The way he'd used Nicole was disgusting enough, but not telling Melanie what he'd done was practically the same as lying.

"Hey, gorgeous," Jesse said with a flirty smile. "How's it going?"

Melanie looked him over, the expression on her face designed to tell him how thoroughly he bored her. Jesse's eyes registered the insult, but he didn't give up. "So. Are you going to the Eight Prime meeting tomorrow?"

"Of course."

"Do you want a ride?"

Melanie stopped walking and reluctantly turned to face Jesse. He obviously realized something was wrong and was trying to charm her back, but she didn't even want to talk to him. Maybe it wasn't her business, but the more she thought about how he'd toyed with Nicole, the more it bothered her. She still remembered too well how it felt to be taken advantage of by a guy. . . .

In that first year after her mother had died, when Melanie thought nothing worse could happen, she'd bounced from guy to guy the way she'd bounced from party to party, just trying to kill the pain. She'd told herself then that the drinking, the smoking, and the random makeout sessions weren't her fault, that she deserved a little comfort. She knew better now. There wasn't any comfort in getting drunk and being lied to for the night—Nicole could vouch for that. When Melanie finally realized the truth, she'd sworn off drinking, drugs, *and* guys. Even so, the thought that Jesse was that type of slime made her coldly furious.

"I can get there myself. I'll walk if I have to."

"You'd rather walk than ride with me?" he demanded, stung.

"Now you're getting the idea."

One guy in particular had really led her on. Jack Bailey had just graduated from CCHS the summer Melanie was looking toward ninth grade, and she'd been sure he was the love of her life. He'd seemed so cool, so sophisticated. . . . She'd lied about her age at first, but when he'd learned the truth, it hadn't mattered. He told her he loved her, that he wanted to be with her forever. And Melanie had believed him . . . had told him she loved him too. . . .

"What's your problem lately, anyway?" Jesse asked angrily. "Why are you acting this way?"

Jack had been lying, of course. In her heart, Melanie suspected that most guys were liars. When the summer was over, Jack had headed off to college without a backward glance. Melanie hated even the thought of him now. The only saving grace was that he'd apparently been too embarrassed by his taste for junior-high girls to brag to his buddies about her. That sad, drunken year had cost her a lot, but, ironically, not her reputation.

"Well?" prompted Jesse.

"Well, what?" Melanie retorted, snapping back to the present.

"I said, why are you acting so cold to me lately?"

Melanie shrugged impatiently. "You're a smart boy," she said, in a tone that implied just the opposite. "Why don't you see if you can figure it out?"

Then, before he could protest further, Melanie stepped through the open door of her classroom and left him behind in the hall.

"After you," Miguel said gallantly, making a production out of waving Leah ahead of him onto the large, broad rock that jutted into the lake.

"Why, thank you." Leah giggled and dropped an

elaborate curtsy before she edged by him and walked to the end of the rock.

Miguel followed, slipping his arms around her waist as they reached the water's edge. "You smell good," he breathed as he brushed his lips over the tender skin at the nape of her neck.

Leah leaned back into him, her half-closed eyes on the green lake water, her mind still half unable to believe they were together. "I think the lake is turning into your favorite spot," she teased.

During the summer, the rustic, tree-shaded lake facilities were mobbed with kids and picnicking families. But once the school year started, it became the number-one makeout spot for teens. Around CCHS, "going to the lake" did *not* mean swimming.

"It's *always* been one of my favorite spots," Miguel replied.

Leah twisted around in his arms, her sculpted eyebrows raised. "Oh, really?"

"No. I mean, not like *that*. Not like *you're* thinking." Miguel quit defending himself and smiled—a half-bemused, completely besotted grin. "I've never met a girl like you for jumping to conclusions."

Leah melted up against him, satisfied. "I'll bet you've never met a girl like me, period."

Miguel answered by kissing her. Leah kissed him back, her arms reaching up to wrap around his neck, her hands burying themselves in the warmth of his hair. The kiss continued until Leah's legs gave out and they sank down onto the rock together, still holding each other tightly, their lips still pressed together. For a while Leah was oblivious to anything else. Then the kiss broke off and gradually she became aware of the sun-warmed surface of the rock radiating heat through the fabric of her jeans and the slight dusting of sand gritting beneath her hips as she wriggled into a sitting position against Miguel. The mildest of breezes ruffled her hair, and she turned her head slightly to watch it play through his. Miguel was so handsome with his thick, dark hair and clear brown eyes. It was amazing to her now how easily she'd once ignored his appearance.

"What are you thinking?" he asked, his smile showing perfect white teeth.

Leah grinned back. "If I tell you, you'll just get conceited."

"Really? In that case, I *definitely* want to hear it."

"Too bad." Leah tucked her head into his shoulder and matched her breathing to his. It was so peaceful on their rock, the tiny ripples of the lake lapping rhythmically around them. Leah could understand why the lake was Miguel's favorite spot. A person could hear herself think there, could let big dreams unfold. She settled back more comfortably in Miguel's embrace, completely happy. "I love it here," she said with a sigh.

"Yeah." Miguel gave her a playful little shove. "It's the company."

"I know," Leah countered. "*You* must be in heaven."

Miguel tried not to laugh and ended up snorting. "You're pretty funny—for an intellectual."

"Ugh. I hate that word. Let's just agree to call me incredibly intelligent and leave it at that."

"Works for me," said Miguel. He buried his face in her hair and kissed the top of her head.

It was a perfect moment. Every bit of the so-called intelligence she'd just been bragging about screamed at her to leave it alone, but Leah didn't listen. "Did you tell your mom about me yet?" she asked.

"Well . . ."

"Miguel! What are you waiting for?"

"Nothing. I'm going to tell her."

"When?"

"Soon."

"*Miguel* . . ." She couldn't believe she was whining. "My parents can't wait to meet *you*."

"Oh?" Miguel sat up straighter, pushing her gently upright. "Why?"

"Because you're my friend." *Oh, what the heck*, she thought. "Actually . . . I've been thinking about telling them you're my boyfriend."

"You have?" Miguel asked, an amazed grin lighting his face.

"Yeah. Why? Is that wrong?"

"No." He seemed pleased, but also strangely shy, and Leah was suddenly reminded how far out of his shell he'd come. At school, or when other people were around, Miguel still used words as if each one were taking ten minutes off his life. But when the two of them were alone he was so different now that Leah forgot how reserved he used to be.

"And your parents . . . they don't mind that my family's Catholic?" Miguel asked, surprising her completely out of her previous train of thought.

"Huh? Of course not. Why would they?"

Miguel shook his head, but his voice sounded relieved as he said, "I don't know. I just thought with your dad being Jewish and . . . what was your mom again?"

"Lutheran—about a hundred years ago. I told you they don't practice."

"I know, but—"

"But nothing. It's so inconsequential it's not even worth mentioning."

Leah felt Miguel's muscles tense where she still leaned up against him. "So then, you didn't tell them."

"Well . . . not exactly," she admitted. "I didn't know it was important."

Miguel shrugged. "You might be surprised how important parents think things like that are."

"Okay, fine. So I'll tell them," she said, trying to

head off the scowl she saw gathering on his face. "Believe me, it won't change a thing."

But the conversation had flustered her. What a weird thing for Miguel to be worried about! Her college-professor parents were the two coolest adults Leah knew. The idea of their judging someone because of his religion was ludicrous. Or because of his parents' religion, really, since Miguel had left the church two years before, when his father died of cancer. Leah couldn't figure out why the subject had come up at all.

*Because he's stalling, that's why,* she realized, a smile edging onto her face. *He's afraid to meet Mom and Dad, because he's afraid they might not like him.*

Leah shook her head. It was really pretty adorable.

Jenna opened the door to her bedroom on Wednesday afternoon and stopped dead in her tracks, unable to believe her eyes.

*Maggie!* she thought, staring open-mouthed. *She said she was going to get even.* But never—not in her worst nightmares—could Jenna have imagined her sister's payback.

*She's going to be so sorry she did this,* Jenna vowed as she walked into the empty room and sat down on her bed. *She must have spent every cent of allowance she's ever saved.*

Maggie's entire side of the room was plastered

with posters of a teeny-bopper band called Clue—Maggie's *entire* side of the room. The posters had been cut to fit like wallpaper where they went around light sockets and switches, and when they reached the ceiling they simply folded over and kept on going—right to the center line between Jenna's and Maggie's halves. Even the end wall of the room, with its large single window, had been papered on Maggie's side. The posters surrounded exactly half of the opening.

Jenna stared with a mixture of shock and admiration. The posters were truly horrible—purple and green and orange. Not only that, Maggie *knew* Jenna couldn't stand Clue. But the kicker, the really brilliant part, was that there wasn't so much as one corner of one poster on Jenna's side of the room. It looked as if her sister had actually measured.

Jenna was still trying to digest the situation when Maggie came bounding through the door with her nose in the air. One look at her older sister's stunned face, though, and her haughty expression dissolved into laughter. She threw herself onto her bed, laughing helplessly, so pleased with herself she could barely stand it.

"I told you I'd get you back," she said smugly when she could speak again.

Jenna was far too angry to reply. At least if one of the posters had been on her side of the room she could have torn it down and ripped it to shreds. But she wasn't going to get even that minor amount of release. And the thought of looking at those putrid posters indefinitely made her want to be sick! She took several deep breaths, then got up and walked out of the room, into the upstairs hall.

"Oh, run and tell Mom," Maggie's voice taunted behind her. "There goes the big high-schooler running for her mommy!"

But unfortunately Jenna didn't want her mother in on the situation any more than Maggie did. If Jenna complained about the posters, it was bound to come out that she'd put her sister's underwear out the window, and Jenna was pretty sure her parents wouldn't understand how completely Maggie had deserved that. Instead, Jenna headed to the linen closet and took out two clean sheets. Then she spun on her heel and marched back into the room she shared with Maggie.

"What are you doing with those sheets?" Maggie asked immediately.

*She looks a lot less sure of herself now*, Jenna noted with satisfaction. Without a word, Jenna crossed from the doorway to her desk and started pulling long metal pushpins out of her cork bulletin board. She gathered a big handful and put them into the front pocket of her loose-fitting pants, then went over to her bed and dropped one of the folded white sheets onto it. With a big, theatrical *crack*, she unfurled the other sheet, snapping it out into the room.

"Mom's going to be mad if you do something to her sheets," Maggie warned. She was fishing. Jenna knew her sister had no idea what she was up to. Yet.

The unfolded sheet in one hand, Jenna grabbed a chair and pulled it over to the window wall. Standing on its seat, she began carefully pinning the plain white cloth to the ceiling, using the edges of Maggie's posters as a guide to make a curtain down the exact center of the room. One after another, Jenna pushed in the pins, getting down to move the chair along as the curtain turned into a room divider. The first sheet stretched not quite halfway across the room. Jenna immediately started on sheet two, pinning it up without a gap.

"You can't leave those up there!" Maggie protested from behind the clean-smelling wall of white.

"Watch me," Jenna muttered, breaking her silence at last. *If you can see me, that is,* she added to herself. This room divider idea was sheer genius. Or not-so-sheer genius, actually. *I should have thought of this a long time ago.*

"It looks stupid," Maggie complained.

"You'd be the expert on that. Anyone who'd spend her money on Clue posters obviously hasn't got one."

"Oh yeah?" Maggie blustered. "Well . . . Well . . .

You're going to have to walk across my side when you want to go in and out."

"I'll survive. But you have no reason *ever* to be on my side, so I'd better not see you over here."

Jenna used her last pushpin and got down from the chair. The two big sheets stretched almost all the way across the room, leaving only a three-foot gap between the end of the second sheet and the wall—a perfect doorway for Jenna to walk through.

"Beautiful," she breathed. It wasn't as good as having her own room, of course, but it was a whole lot better than looking at Maggie. In fact, the divider made it *almost* possible to imagine that the little creep wasn't even there.

"Amen," said the Altmanns in unison.

Peter lifted his head and opened his eyes, grateful for the food on the table in front of him. He never forgot for a second anymore how lucky he was to live in a nice, safe home with plenty to eat and parents who loved him. Those basic, everyday things— things he'd once taken for granted—had assumed new value in Peter's eyes through his work with the Junior Explorers.

"Everything looks delicious," Mr. Altmann said, winking at his wife. "Tuna casserole—my favorite."

"Oh, Henry. You know that's pasta primavera!" Mrs. Altmann scolded. "You had it before and you said you liked it."

"Did I?"

Peter smiled. His dad was forever misidentifying everything on the table. It was a game he played that Peter's mother never seemed to catch on to.

"Yes. You had it at the last potluck and made such a big fuss about it that I asked Alice Chapman for the recipe."

"I remember now," Mr. Altmann said, heaping pasta onto his plate with a barely suppressed twinkle in his eyes. "Everyone was raving about Alice's possum primavera."

"Oh, you," his wife groaned good-naturedly, finally realizing she'd been taken in again.

"Here, Dad, have a muffin," Peter offered, passing his father the dinner rolls.

"You're *both* terrible," Mrs. Altmann declared.

Peter knew that if his brother, David, hadn't been away at college, he'd probably have gotten a gag out of the salad somehow. Joking about the food was just a backhanded way of showing their mother how much they liked her cooking.

The three of them passed the various dishes around while the sky outside the windows darkened gradually into night. Peter's parents talked about the events of the day, but Peter chewed absently, his mind on Jenna. There was something about his best friend that seemed a little off lately—a little bit unhappy. He couldn't put his finger on it, but he hoped it wasn't anything *he'd* done.

*Maybe she's pining away for you, hoping you'll make the big move,* he thought, wishing he had any reason at all to believe that. He couldn't even entertain the idea as a reasonable fantasy. *Well, what then?*

He had no idea.

"You're awfully quiet tonight, Peter," his mother said, interrupting his thoughts. "Is everything all right?"

"Huh? Oh, sure. Of course."

"Something on your mind?" Mr. Altmann asked.

"Maybe," Peter admitted reluctantly, not wanting to discuss it. "Nothing bad, though."

His mom looked relieved.

"How's it going with Eight Prime?" his father asked. "Are they still coming over tomorrow night?"

"Yep. We're going to talk about our next fundraiser."

"I'm so proud of you kids," Mrs. Altmann told him. "Especially you, Peter. The Junior Explorers are lucky to have you."

Peter was pleased but also embarrassed. "I don't know about that."

"No, your mother's right," said Mr. Altmann. "I've been thinking about it, though, Peter, and you ought to make use of the church on this bus drive. The congregation's ready to stand behind you and Chris with the Junior Explorers program anytime you say the word. People want to help—show them how they can."

"What do you mean?"

"I mean include the church in your fund-raisers. Let us help you earn the money. Someone in the congregation might have a line on a bus you could buy, too. Adults have connections that teens don't know about. Use them."

Peter considered this. "Not everyone in Eight Prime belongs to a church. A couple of people weren't too thrilled when Jenna suggested we call our group the Christian Youth Association."

"But they stuck with you anyway," Peter's mother pointed out, "so they must really want to help those children. How could they possibly object to a little extra boost from your friends?"

"We're not telling you what to do, son," his father added quickly. "We think you're doing a great job on your own. I'm just suggesting there's a whole big resource out there ready and eager to be tapped. The church facilities, for example. You might be able to use the parking lot, or even the buildings, if you ask Reverend Thompson. And if you ever needed adults for anything, your mother and I'd volunteer in a heartbeat—and so would a lot of other people at church. That's all I'm saying."

Peter nodded slowly. "Thanks. It would be easier in some ways if everyone in the group was a Christian. But I'll tell you something—I don't think the way Eight Prime came together was an accident.

I've prayed about it, and I really think the group was meant to be exactly how it is."

"The Lord *does* work in mysterious ways," Mrs. Altmann said.

"Yeah," Peter agreed with a grin. "That's one of the things I like about him."

The rest of dinner passed quickly. Peter helped clear the table and wash the dishes, then went to his room to do some homework. As soon as he was alone again, his mind returned to Jenna.

*Maybe I should have told my parents how my feelings for Jenna have changed*, he thought. *They might have had some good advice*. But the idea of discussing something like that with his parents just seemed too weird.

*Still . . . Mom and Dad were best friends before they got married. You could have just casually asked them how they knew it when their friendship became love.*

Groaning, Peter threw himself backward onto his bed. With a question that obvious, he might as well draw them a map.

What he needed was a plan. A *firm* plan. He needed to figure out *exactly* what to say—maybe even write it down—and then he needed to figure out exactly when and where to say it.

"I could ask her on a date," he murmured, thinking aloud. "Only I won't *call* it a date. But I'll take her somewhere nice. Somewhere *romantic*. And then I'll tell her how much she means to me. . . . Maybe buy her flowers or something . . ."

The idea had possibilities. He'd have to work on it, but it might pan out. In any event, now that he'd at least decided to do things in an organized way, he wouldn't feel as if he had to keep watching for any spare moment alone with her to blurt out his deepest feelings. He could enjoy Jenna's company again without worrying every second.

Until he finalized his plan, of course. After that he'd be worrying plenty.

# Six

"Are you sure about this, Vanessa?" Melanie asked nervously, eyeing the minitrampoline. "I don't want to sound like a baby, but it doesn't seem very safe."

Vanessa crossed her arms and looked put out. "Red River is doing it, and they're practically the least-coordinated squad in the district."

That last part wasn't true, but Red River *was* CCHS's biggest rival, which made most of the cheerleaders feel the need to trash them on a regular basis. Even Melanie didn't like the idea of coming in second to that particular squad, with its full-time coach and matching attitude.

"Oh, *that's* what we need," Tiffany drawled sarcastically. "Humiliation at the hands of Red River. I can't wait."

"Who said we're going to get humiliated?" Melanie demanded, her pride aroused. "I was only asking."

"I have to agree with Melanie—it *doesn't* seem very safe," Tanya put in. "What's to keep her from going right over the top of the pyramid? She's going to be landing blind after she does that flip. If she misses her footing or can't check her rotation, she's going to fall and go splat on her face."

Tanya's dead-accurate analysis of Vanessa's new stunt didn't do much to put Melanie at ease. She glanced at the trampoline again and tried to envision herself actually doing what her squad leader had proposed. Vanessa had told her to run hard, bounce off the trampoline, do a forward flip in the air, and land on her feet at the top of the spirit pyramid. The cheerleaders at CCHS made their pyramid with three girls on hands and knees in the bottom row and two girls on top of them. When Melanie landed—*if* she landed—she would complete the peak with one foot in the middle of Tiffany's back and one on Cindy White's.

*That's actually the best part of the whole thing*, Melanie thought with a sideways glance at Tiffany. *I should have worn my soccer cleats*.

"There's nothing to be afraid of," Vanessa argued. "If Melanie accidentally overshoots the pyramid, Lou Anne and Tanya will be in front to catch her." Tanya and Lou Anne were normally stationed behind the pyramid, to catch Melanie when she fell backward in the dismount, but now they were moving out front.

"So who's going to catch her if she falls *backward*?" Angela asked, beating Melanie to the question.

"There's no way she's going to fall backward," Lou Anne snorted. "Think about it. All her momentum is going to be going forward. The worst thing that can happen is she won't land well and she'll keep on coming. Then Tanya and I will catch her. It's perfectly safe."

*Yeah. For you*, Melanie couldn't help thinking. Even so, she was getting excited. She loved to do difficult stunts, and she was usually pretty fearless. The danger factor in this one had taken her by surprise, but the more she thought about it, the more convinced she was becoming that she could do it. The first couple of times were bound to be a little heart-stopping, but there were good thick crash pads on the gymnasium floor. And once she had it down, what a rush! Melanie imagined doing the stunt in front of packed bleachers at the next football game.

*Besides, if Red River is doing it . . .*

"Okay, form up," she said decisively. "If we're going to do this thing, let's do it."

The other girls stared like zombies. Even Vanessa looked shocked.

*She didn't think I'd do it*, Melanie realized. A slow smile curved her lips. *She doesn't know me as well as she thought she did.*

"So, are we on for this or what?" she asked, looking directly at Vanessa.

The squad leader snapped out of her stupor and clapped her hands together loudly. "Come on, let's go!" she shouted. "Form up."

The other girls hustled to form the spirit pyramid. A moment later Melanie's entire world had contracted into a minitrampoline and the bent backs of the two girls she was supposed to land on. She hesitated a second, then started to run.

*Don't think about it—just hit it hard,* she told herself as her feet struck the spongy-taut surface of the trampoline and she sprang up through the air. She had lots of speed, plenty of height. She tucked and flipped so quickly that it was over almost before she knew she was starting. She was coming out of the flip, her legs straightening, reaching down for something solid to land on. With a shuddering impact, her feet found Tiffany, striking her squarely in the back. Melanie teetered at the top of the pyramid for one brief, unstable instant; then the whole thing began to collapse.

"Jump!" Tanya shouted, reaching up to grab her by the hand and guide her forward to safety. Melanie jumped and, with Tanya's help, landed gracefully just as Tiffany fell off the pyramid and hit the crash mat in a heap. Cindy tumbled off in the other direction, and the three girls on the bottom row rose to their feet. Nobody was hurt.

"You're supposed to land on *both* of us," Tiffany complained bitterly from the mat. "Not just me."

"Sorry," Melanie said innocently. "Do you need a hand getting up?"

She had a feeling she was going to like this stunt after all.

Nicole turned a page of her new fashion magazine and immediately sat straight up on the bed.

" 'Are you a U.S. Girl?' " she read aloud, her heart pounding as excitedly as when she'd first seen the poster two days before. "Oh, wow, they're advertising in magazines now!"

Nicole flopped back onto her pillows and tried to imagine girls all across the country opening this same magazine and seeing this same ad. It was a mental picture that didn't come easily. Nicole knew she had no idea how big the rest of the country really was—it was one of the major irritations of her existence. "It's not my fault I've spent my entire life in stupid Clearwater Crossing," she muttered discontentedly.

Then her mind began to wander. In her daydream, Nicole saw herself wowing the judges in St. Louis. Would they have a tiara for the winner, she wondered, like in the Miss America contest? Nicole could get used to the idea of herself in a tiara—maybe carrying one of those enormous bouquets of red roses. She put a hand to her head, adjusting the diamonds that weren't there, then tossed her blond hair and began her imagined victory walk down the runway. What a triumph! The crowd loved her, yelling and cheering, while the other contestants smiled those totally fake I'm-so-happy-for-you smiles and hated her behind her back. Nicole sighed happily. *Wouldn't that be great?* she thought.

She threw the magazine aside and hurried to her desk, retrieving the contest entry blank from the top drawer. The two-sided form had more information than the magazine advertisement did. It told prospective contestants exactly what they had to wear (any brand of jeans, with red, white, and blue for the rest of the outfit), where they had to go (the enormous Skyline Mall in St. Louis for Missouri residents), how to sign up (either in advance, by mailing in the form, or at the mall on the day of the event), and about the final contest (to be held in Hollywood!) to select five girls from the winners in the fifty states.

Nicole put the entry blank down, then opened her closet and took out a plastic U.S. Girls shopping bag. Placing it carefully on her rumpled bed, she loosened the drawstring and extracted the precisely folded jeans she'd bought on Tuesday. She held them up for examination, the legs unfurling as she did.

"These are so cute," she whispered, wondering if she could get into them yet. Without even trying them on, Nicole had decided to buy the jeans one size smaller than the pair she'd barely squeezed into at the store. Since only two days had gone by, it didn't seem likely the pants would fit yet, but she decided to try anyway. Hurriedly checking to see that the door between her room and the bathroom she shared with her thirteen-year-old sister, Heather, was locked, Nicole stripped off the pants and lace-trimmed T-shirt she'd worn to school, then stood in front of the full-length mirror in her underwear. A satisfied smile lit her eyes.

"You're getting seriously thin," she said out loud, admiring the view. It hadn't come easy, that was for sure. She'd dieted all summer just to lose ten pounds, but she'd lost another four since school had started. Her hip bones were clearly visible now, even when she was standing up.

Holding her breath, Nicole stepped into her new jeans and tried to pull them up. They came as far as the knees without resistance, but partway up the thigh, things got tight in a hurry. Nicole had to work to get them all the way up her legs—getting them over her hips to her waist was nearly impossible. "Oh, wow," she gasped. It felt as if she were wearing a girdle, and the pants weren't even buttoned yet. Nicole eyed the V-shaped expanse of white belly showing through the gap of her open fly and felt herself beginning to panic. There was no way those pants were closing. Not today. Not next week. Not the week after that . . .

"Stop it!" she said out loud, taking a deep breath. The contest was still four weeks away. That gave her plenty of time to diet. She'd just have to be smart about this—she'd have to stop eating completely.

*Because you have to win this contest*, she thought. She'd known that almost from the moment she'd first seen the poster. She *had* to win, because this was her chance to fix everything. When she was a famous model, her entire life would change for the better: her stupid little sister would show her some respect, her parents would have to give her more freedom and let her see the world, and at school she'd finally be popular. Not a little bit, oh-yeah-I-know-who-she-is popular, the way she was now. *Mega*popular. Melanie Andrews popular.

But the best thing of all would be the chance to laugh in Jesse Jones's face. How she ached to pay him back for the way he'd treated her! How she'd love to saunter by him in the quad with an adoring guy on either side of her and a whole smitten squad following along behind. *Cute* guys . . . no, *college* guys . . . no, *fellow models*! Wouldn't that just serve him right?

Nicole smiled at the image. When she got famous, she was going to pretend she didn't even know who Jesse Jones was.

"Okay, then. I guess I'll see you in a couple of hours," Peter said as he steered his blue Toyota to the curb in front of Jenna's house.

"Well, yeah." *Obviously* he'd see her—the Eight

Prime meeting was at his house that night. Jenna got out of the car and pulled her backpack onto one shoulder, then slammed the passenger door. "Later," she called, waving through the window. Peter nodded and drove off.

*He sure is acting strange lately*, Jenna thought, watching him go. *Almost as if I make him nervous or something*. All afternoon, while the two of them worked on homework in his den, he'd been jumpy and distracted. Jenna had asked him a question about geometry and he'd nearly knocked over his soda. She'd never seen him that way before, and she didn't think she liked it.

The Conrads' front door flew open, startling her out of her trance. "Jenna! Hurry up!" her ten-year-old sister, Sarah, yelled. "Mom's putting dinner on the table!"

"Oops!" Jenna turned and ran up the walkway, her long hair streaming out behind her. She'd gotten home a little late, but she still wanted to put her things in her room and wash up before everyone sat down.

"Thanks, squirt," she said as she shot by her sister and up the staircase. With seven people in the house to plan meals around, Mrs. Conrad didn't take kindly to anyone coming to the table late. Jenna knew she'd have to hurry.

She reached the top of the stairs, flung her door open, and froze. Her chest clenched so tightly with anger that for a moment she couldn't breathe. Maggie's stupid Clue posters were all exactly as Jenna had left them, but the little weasel had taken down her sheets! Every single pushpin had been pulled from the ceiling, and they weren't back in her bulletin board, either. They were gone, like the sheets. Vanished without a trace.

"Oh, this really tears it!" Jenna exclaimed, forgetting that she'd wanted to wash up for dinner, forgetting everything except getting even with Maggie. "I don't have to put up with this!" She dropped her backpack, turned, and raced down the stairs, bursting into the dining room just as the rest of her family was gathering to eat.

"Don't let us keep you waiting," her father teased as she slid ungracefully into her usual seat.

Jenna bit her lip while she waited for her parents, Caitlin, Maggie, Allison, and Sarah to sit down. She had every intention of calling Maggie's bluff within the next five minutes, but she knew better than to do it before grace. Everyone bowed their heads.

"Dear Lord, for the food on this table, we thank you," Mr. Conrad began, reciting the prayer his father had taught him as a boy. "For the people in this room, we thank you. And for the love and forgiveness you've shown us, we thank you with all our hearts."

"Amen," said the Conrads in unison.

Then people started passing plates, and Jenna couldn't wait a second longer. "Why'd you take those sheets down?" she demanded, glaring at Maggie across the wooden table. "I told you not to touch those."

"I *didn't* take them down," Maggie returned smugly as she helped herself to an enormous serving of scalloped potatoes. "So there."

Jenna was so angry that she didn't stop even a second to consider what her sister had said. "Oh, right," she returned sarcastically. "Aliens probably snuck into our room and used them to build a weather balloon."

"Interesting possibility," Mrs. Conrad said. "Or perhaps it was just your mother. By the way, dear, can you help me launch that weather balloon after dinner?" she asked, winking at her husband.

Maggie tossed her auburn curls, a triumphant glint in her eyes, and for the first time in Jenna's life she felt an almost overpowering urge to smack her.

"Told ya," Maggie gloated.

"Stop it, Maggie," Mr. Conrad said quietly.

Jenna knew she was on shaky ground. Every bit of her common sense told her to let the subject drop, but she couldn't. It wasn't fair.

"How come you took down my sheets but not Maggie's ugly posters?" she demanded, turning to her mother. "Why can't I have a room divider if I want one?"

"Well, in the first place, Jenna, I thought your little divider was very mean-spirited—"

"Did you *see* the posters?" Jenna interrupted hotly. "What could be more mean-spirited than plastering someone's room with a band as stupid as Clue?"

"In the second place," Mrs. Conrad continued calmly, "my sheets are not at your disposal. They're for the *beds*, and I'll thank you to ask me the next time you get the urge to use one for some other purpose."

"Mom!" Jenna protested. "I shouldn't have to share a room with Maggie in the first place! Caitlin should move out!"

There was a stunned, split-second silence around the table. Even Jenna was shocked by how rude she'd just been.

"That's enough!" Mrs. Conrad snapped, her eyes flashing. "I'm disappointed in you, Jenna. I didn't think you could be so uncharitable."

Jenna risked a glance at Caitlin. Her sister's eyes were on her plate. "I didn't mean—" she began lamely.

"That's all right," Caitlin said quickly. "I understand."

"I think you need to work on your attitude, Jenna," her father told her. His voice was firm but not unkind. "I know being sixteen isn't easy, but it isn't impossible either. Just remember the Golden Rule."

*Easy for you to say,* Jenna thought rebelliously. *You don't share a room with Maggie!* Some part of her heart knew her parents were right, that she should be more forgiving of her sisters, but she wasn't ready to listen just then. Instead she glared across the table at Maggie, who grinned back like the Cheshire cat. Jenna was positive the little twerp was congratulating herself on winning the divider war and getting Jenna in trouble to boot. Somehow Jenna had come off looking like the bad guy while Little Miss Maggie was polishing her halo. *This is not over,* Jenna vowed silently, plotting revenge.

"Guess what? I have a date for the Fall Fantasy," Maggie announced to the table. "It's Scott Jenner!"

"No way!" seventh-grader Allison shrieked. "Did you ask him, or did he ask you?"

"*He* asked *me.* Isn't it exciting? I can go, can't I, Mom?"

The Fall Fantasy was the eighth-grade formal, and Maggie had been aching to go to it since the very first day of sixth grade. Whenever she mentioned it, she acted as if it were Cinderella's ball at the palace. Her crush on Scott Jenner went back further still, and, as far as Jenna knew, this was the first time he'd so much as glanced her way. Maggie's freckled face glowed with the thrill of it all as she looked to her parents for permission.

⇒ clearwater crossing ⇐

Dear *Clearwater Crossing* Reader,

**Your opinion counts!** Please answer the following questions and return this card after you have read the book. Be completely honest—there are no right or wrong answers. No stamp is necessary, just drop the card in any mailbox. Thanks!

**1. Did you like this book?** (Check one)
☑ I loved it ☐ I liked it ☐ It was OK ☐ I didn't like it ☐ I hated it

**2. How did you find out about this book?** (Check one)
☐ *Teen* magazine ☐ *Brio* magazine ☐ In-store sampler ☐ Radio advertisements ☐ Bookstore ☐ In-store Display
☐ Ad in a Lurlene McDaniel book ☐ Friend ☑ Other (Please specify) Wal-Mart

**3. Would you read another *Clearwater Crossing* book?** (Check one)
☐ Definitely Yes ☑ Probably Yes ☐ Maybe ☐ Probably Not ☐ Definitely Not

**4. Please rank the following in order of importance to you in deciding to buy this book** (1 being most important, 6 being least):
_2_ Subject/content _4_ Cover ___ Friend recommended _3_ Back of book copy _1_ Read preview sampler ___ Advertisement

**5. Would you recommend *Clearwater Crossing* to a friend?** (Check one)
☐ Definitely Yes ☑ Probably Yes ☐ Maybe ☐ Probably Not ☐ Definitely Not

**6. Where did you buy this book?**
☐ Walden ☐ Borders ☐ Barnes & Noble ☐ Religious bookstore (Store name) _____ ☐ Other bookstore
☐ Discount store (like K-Mart) ☐ Grocery store ☐ Received as a gift ☑ Other (Please specify) Wal-Mart

**7. Who picked out this book?** (Check one)
☑ I did ☐ Friend ☐ Parent/Grandparent ☐ Other (Please specify) My sister

**8. Who paid for this book?** (Check one)
☑ I did ☐ Friend ☐ Parent/Grandparent ☐ Other (Please specify) My sister

**9. Which of these books/series do you like to read?** (Check all that apply)
☑ Lurlene McDaniel ☐ PCU ☐ Christy ☐ Cedar River Daydreams ☑ Sierra Jensen
☑ Love Stories ☑ Other Lots

**10. Do you belong to a Christian or church youth group?** ☑ Yes ☐ No   If yes, what is the name of the group? Apostolic Bible Croorr

**11. On a scale of 1-10 (1 is worst, 10 is best), how does *Clearwater Crossing* rank as a series?** ___

**12. Which, if any, of these magazines do you read regularly?** (Check all that apply)
☐ YM ☐ Teen ☐ Brio ☐ Seventeen ☐ You! ☐ Youth 97

Reader's Name _____ Date of Birth ___/___/___

Address _____ City _____ State _____ Zip _____

CCS#1

# BUSINESS REPLY MAIL

FIRST-CLASS MAIL    PERMIT NO. 01239    NEW YORK, NY

POSTAGE WILL BE PAID BY ADDRESSEE

**BANTAM DOUBLEDAY DELL**
BOOKS FOR YOUNG READERS
SERIES MARKETING
1540 Broadway
New York  NY  10109-1225

NO POSTAGE
NECESSARY
IF MAILED
IN THE
UNITED STATES

*So what?* Jenna thought angrily, refusing to be impressed. *Big deal.*

"I don't see why not," Mrs. Conrad said. "As long as it's properly chaperoned."

"And I'll want to drive you and pick you up myself," Mr. Conrad added. "You can meet Scott there. When's the dance?"

"On Friday, a week from tomorrow," said Maggie, beaming as if she'd just invented chocolate. "I can't wait!"

*So what?* Jenna repeated to herself. She stabbed viciously at a piece of ham. *Yippee.*


"No more car washes," Jenna pronounced in a decidedly grumpy tone. "Let's do something else this time."

Peter looked askance at her before turning his attention back to the rest of the group in his living room. Jenna seemed to be in an even worse mood now than she'd been in that afternoon.

"Let's sell something," Jesse suggested. "That's easier than washing cars."

Jenna smiled at him appreciatively.

"What should we sell?" asked Ben.

"Seasonal things sell well," Leah mused. "If it were later in the year, we could sell Christmas decorations, or wreaths. . . ."

"October is only a week away," Melanie pointed out. "How about something for Halloween?"

"Like what?" asked Nicole. "The only thing anyone buys for Halloween is candy, and since we can't get it cheaper than anyone else, how would we make a profit?"

"No, wait," Peter said, an idea starting to form. "What about pumpkins?"

"*Pumpkins?*" Jesse repeated. "Produce wasn't exactly what I had in mind."

"Think about it a minute, Jesse," Peter insisted. "Nearly every family buys at least one to make a jack-o'-lantern. If we buy a lot of them, we might find a good deal at a farm somewhere. Then we could sell them at a profit."

"A *farm?*" Jesse said the word as if he'd never heard it before.

"Welcome to Missouri, surfer dude," Melanie muttered under her breath.

*What's wrong with everyone tonight?* Peter wondered.

"The Ozarks are practically famous for their pumpkin crop," Jenna told Jesse. "I think Peter has a good idea."

"Let's sell them at school," Melanie suggested. "We could sell them in the quad during lunch."

"That'll be fun!" Ben said excitedly.

"I don't *think* so!" Nicole broke in. "Could you all maybe think of something *more* embarrassing?" She and Melanie locked antagonistic stares across the room.

"I agree with Nicole," said Jesse. "We don't need to do this at school."

Instead of thanking him, Nicole tossed her head and looked away, out the darkened window.

Peter felt as if the group was disintegrating before his eyes, but he didn't know what to say. He didn't have the slightest idea why they all seemed so impatient with each other.

"I don't see what the big deal about selling pumpkins at school is," Miguel put in. "It doesn't embarrass *me*. I do think we'll need special permission, though. Probably from the principal."

"You're right," Jesse said, sitting up straighter in his armchair. "Melanie and I should do that together."

Peter blinked. Hadn't Jesse just said he didn't want to sell things on campus? Now he was itching to ask for permission.

"After all, Melanie and I are kind of the campus leaders," Jesse went on. "I think Principal Kelly will be more likely to let us hold the sale if we're the ones who ask him."

"Ask him yourself," said Melanie.

Raw irritation flicked across Jesse's features. "I think it would make a much better impression if we *both*—"

"I don't think so, Jesse." The two glared at each other.

"I'll ask Principal Kelly if you want," Leah volunteered in the silence that followed. "My parents know him, so it's no big deal. I'm sure he'll say yes."

"Thanks, Leah," Peter accepted gratefully. "And maybe Jenna and I can start looking for a deal on pumpkins this weekend. We'll drive to a few farms and check out their prices. Okay, Jenna?"

"Sure," Jenna said absently. For some reason she was staring at Leah, who was sitting in her usual place beside Miguel.

"Okay. That's settled then," Peter said, feeling as if he'd just negotiated a nuclear arms treaty instead of a pumpkin sale.

*Well, at least we agreed on a plan,* he thought, trying to focus on the positive.

And speaking of the positive, hadn't Jenna just agreed to drive all over the countryside with him this weekend?

*Okay, so we're only shopping for pumpkins. But with the leaves starting to turn colors and the first fall in the air, it* could *be pretty romantic.*

# Seven

"Wait!" Mr. Smythe shouted as the end-of-class bell rang and thirty-two students clattered gratefully to their feet. "I haven't assigned your homework yet."

Jenna joined in the heartfelt groan that echoed around the classroom. She usually liked her teachers, but her English teacher this year, Mr. Smythe, was turning out to be awful.

There was his name, for one thing. Everyone said it was really Smith, but that he'd changed it to make it sound British. And then there was the way he talked, and the way he paced around in that practiced little circle, and those corduroy jackets with the leather elbow patches, and the Sherlock Holmes pipe he made sure was always on his desk—even though teachers couldn't smoke in the classrooms and he was *exactly* the kind of guy who'd love to give a student detention for smoking anywhere. In a word, he was a prig. Jenna tried not to judge him, but it was hard sometimes.

"I'm waiting for your attention," he told the

fidgeting class, obviously enjoying himself. Some of the students sat back down; most stayed on their feet.

This latest episode was just like Mr. Smythe too—waiting until after the last bell on a Friday to assign his homework. And Jenna knew he would take his sweet time about it, because no one could claim he was making them late for the next class.

"I want you all to write a paper. Three pages, typed, double-spaced," he announced.

There was another mutinous groan.

"Very well. *Five* pages," he amended with a smirk. "The weekend is here, so you'll all have plenty of time."

"They're going to find that guy's body at the bottom of a river someday," the jock behind Jenna muttered under cover of the outraged shouts that followed. "And no one will rat out the killer."

"People, people," Mr. Smythe said, holding up a hand for silence. "Where are your manners? After all, this *is* creative writing. You're supposed to *want* to write."

"What's the rest of the assignment?" a girl's voice called impatiently. "I have to catch a bus."

Mr. Smythe sighed, as if his class's lack of interest truly pained him. "Oh, very well. I want you all to write about a feeling. A *strong* feeling. Explore your emotions—plumb your soul. In other words, don't give me drivel."

"Or maybe at the side of the highway . . . ," the

athlete continued under his breath. Jenna wasn't sure he even knew he was talking out loud.

"What *about* a strong feeling?" Angela Maldonado asked.

Mr. Smythe looked at her as if she were a total idiot. "Why, how it *feels*, of course."

There was more groaning and grumbling as the students made their way through the classroom door and into the hall. Jenna was supposed to meet her mother in the parking lot to help with the grocery shopping, but she had to pick up some things in her locker first. She hurried along as fast as she could against the traffic in the hallway, trying to make up the time Mr. Smythe had wasted. As she did, she mulled over his last-minute assignment.

*Write about a strong feeling,* she thought, rolling her eyes. *Where do teachers get these things?* Still, she didn't really mind. She was a good writer, and formulaic assignments like Mr. Smythe's were usually easy for her.

*Besides,* she added, a wry expression on her face, *finding a strong feeling shouldn't be a problem for me right now. Love, jealousy, anger, frustration. Take your pick—I've got them all.*

When cheering practice let out on Friday, Melanie found Peter waiting for her under one of the big shade trees near the corner of the gym.

"Hi," he called, waving and walking toward her.

97

She met him halfway. "Hi. What are you doing here?"

"I wanted to talk to you. I thought I might be able to catch you alone here."

"Alone? Why?" Melanie asked apprehensively.

"I wanted to ask you about an idea I had for the Eight Prime pumpkin sale. I'm afraid you're not going to like it, but I wanted to ask you anyway."

"Ask me what?" They were walking across campus now, taking slow steps toward the student parking lot. No one stayed after school on Friday if they could avoid it, and Peter and Melanie had the grounds practically to themselves.

"Well, by now you know that Jenna and I are pretty involved in our church. Everyone in the congregation knows about the Junior Explorers, and my dad thinks they'd want to help us earn the bus—*if* we give them the chance."

"Uh-huh." Her voice was calm, but her heart pounded. She already felt weird about being the only atheist in Eight Prime, and the way the conversation was going so far wasn't making her feel any better.

"I just thought maybe we could have *two* pumpkin sales," Peter told her. "We'll do the sale here at school, like we said. But I was hoping we could do another sale, too—in our church parking lot after services one Sunday. I'm pretty sure people would buy a lot of pumpkins if it helped the Junior Explorers. And not only could we sell more, we might get a better price from the farmer, too, since we'll be buying more to start with. We could win two ways." Peter spoke more and more quickly as he came to the end of his explanation, and his eyes were full of conviction. "Would it bother you to have a sale in our church parking lot?"

"Of course not!" Melanie said, laughing with relief. *Was that all he wanted?* "I'm not a fanatic—I just don't believe in God. I'm pretty sure no one will get struck by lightning, though, if I set foot in the parking lot."

Peter smiled. "You don't *have* to stay in the parking lot, you know. You'd be welcome to come to services beforehand."

Melanie grimaced. "Don't push your luck."

"You can't blame me for trying," Peter returned with a mischievous grin.

They had reached the edge of campus. "Can I drive you home?" he offered. "My car's right over there."

"That would be great." She wouldn't be able to invite Peter in, of course—not with her dad the way he was lately—but she was still happy to skip the bus trip.

They crossed the student parking lot to Peter's car and climbed in.

"You'll have to tell me where I'm going. I don't know where you live," Peter said. Melanie gave him brief directions before they lapsed into their separate thoughts. Peter drove through the traffic in silence.

"Did you ever go to church?" he asked after a while. "When you were little, I mean."

"Not really," she said.

"Your parents don't believe in God either?"

"My father is the most determined atheist you'll ever meet. It's practically a religion with him." Melanie chuckled as she recognized the paradox in what she'd just said. "You know what I mean."

"Yeah. I do," Peter said thoughtfully. "I've been thinking about that a lot lately, actually. I think atheism taken past a certain point becomes a type of faith all its own—even if it's not a very comforting one."

"My dad would say the comfort comes from knowing you're right."

Peter smiled ironically. "And *my* dad would say that if your dad's right, he'll never have the satisfaction of knowing it."

Melanie blinked as the truth of Peter's words sank in. Even so, that didn't make him right—not about anything else, anyway. She shrugged. "It's just reality."

"Yeah? Well. No disrespect, but it might be time for a reality check."

Melanie tried to smile but couldn't—the old sadness had suddenly gripped her again. She had really begun to like Peter and, strangely enough, she respected him too. In her heart, though, Melanie knew that she and Peter could never be friends. Not *good* friends. They weren't just from different social circles—they were practically from different worlds. Worlds with nothing in common. The few times Melanie had brushed up against Peter's side of the universe, she'd ended up learning that the hard way.

"Sometimes I wish I *could* believe in God," she admitted with a sigh. "I think life would be easier if I did."

Peter seemed surprised. His eyes left the road a moment to search hers. "What's stopping you?"

"You have to be brought up believing that stuff. *You* believe it because your parents believe it, and your best friend believes it, and everyone you know tells you it's true. It's like it's in your blood now. For me, it's exactly the opposite. For me to start believing in God at this point would take a miracle. Literally. Someone would have to prove to me that he exists."

Peter shook his head. "There are lots of things that can't be proven. Love, for instance. If you had to, do you think you could prove that love exists? Probably not. But you know it does. Because you've felt it, right? I can't prove God exists either, but I know he does. And for the same reason . . . because I've felt him."

Melanie twisted around in her seat. "That's

exactly what I'm talking about. It's all so simple for you."

"It could be simple for you, too, if you let it. Believing in God is a choice people make. You can believe, Melanie. You just have to decide that you want to."

Melanie turned away, gazing out her window as the tawny fields rolled by. "I'm afraid someone already made that choice for me. They made it for you, too—you just don't know it yet."

There was a moment of silence. "Maybe," Peter conceded. "Maybe when I was little. But when I got old enough to understand, I could have changed my mind anytime."

"Maybe."

"You can change your mind too. Just remember that."


Leah poured the delicate china cup two-thirds full of coffee and topped it off with cream, watching as the thick white liquid sank to the bottom, then swirled lazily upward again. The Rosenthals normally drank their after-dinner coffee black, so cream was a rare treat.

"I'm done with the arts section, if you want it," Leah's mother said, handing her part of the newspaper. Leah's father still had a grip on the front news section and was trying to hide the funny pages in his lap.

"Thanks." Leah took the paper and opened it up on the small dining table. She wanted to read it, wanted to settle into the familiar evening routine, but there was something she wanted to get off her chest first.

"You know that guy I told you about before? Miguel?" she blurted out. "Well, anyway . . . we're seeing a lot of each other now—Miguel and I, I mean. I thought you'd want to know."

Her mother smiled and set her coffee cup on the table. "This is your friend on the water polo team?"

To her own amazement, Leah felt herself blushing. She usually told her parents everything, but her relationship with Miguel was still so new, so precious, and they were the very first people to know. "Yes. Well . . . actually, he's kind of my boyfriend now. It's official."

"Your boyfriend!" Mr. Rosenthal exclaimed, slipping into instant Dad mode. "I'm afraid to ask how you make something like that official."

"Dad!" Leah protested.

"Your boyfriend," her mother repeated. "We haven't even met the boy!"

"No. But I've told you about him. And I *want* you to meet him. I was thinking maybe we could all go to brunch together some Sunday."

"That would be nice," her mother said immediately, and Leah suppressed a smile. Mrs. Rosenthal liked to call brunch her only vice, which was the reason Leah had suggested it in the first place.

"All right," her father agreed, if less enthusiastically. "I want to meet this boy now. Anyone who's dating my daughter had better know what he's up against."

"Oh, Dad." Leah giggled. "He's nice. You'll like him."

And then it seemed that everything had been said. Everything except that one little detail. . . .

"By the way, he's Catholic."

Leah winced as her words fell into a sudden silence. That hadn't come out smoothly at all. "He doesn't go to church anymore," she hurried to add. "But he thought you'd want to know."

Mr. Rosenthal's expression was blank. "Why?"

"I don't know. I told him it wouldn't matter one way or the other, but he seemed to think it might."

Mr. Rosenthal shook his head. "Well, I admire his honesty, anyway."

The coolness of his tone took Leah by surprise. "You *don't* care, do you, Dad?"

"Of course not." He hesitated, then buried his face in his paper again.

Leah looked at her mother.

"No. Why should we?" Mrs. Rosenthal reassured her. "We're dying to meet your Miguel. How about next weekend?"

# *Eight*

Peter gripped the steering wheel hard as he guided the car along a thickly wooded country road. It was a gorgeous Saturday afternoon. The sun filtered down through the bright autumn leaves, which fluttered and swirled in the lightest of breezes, and every now and then a ground squirrel or rabbit darted out onto the pavement, scurrying for the brushy cover on the other side.

"It's so pretty out." Jenna sighed, sinking back into the passenger seat. "I'm glad we're doing this today."

"Yeah, me too." Peter knew he *ought* to be glad, anyway, but with everything else on his mind, it was hard to stay focused on pumpkins.

When he'd picked Jenna up a half hour before, she'd been arguing with Maggie. She'd flung herself into his car in a huff and told him all about the ugly posters Maggie had put up in their room, how *she* had ended up in trouble for it, and what a pain in the rear sisters were in general. Peter had listened in silence, struggling to keep a smile off his face. So *that* was what was eating Jenna lately—sharing a room with Maggie. It wasn't anything to do with him. It wasn't even very important!

Peter had wanted to laugh with relief, but the sensation hadn't lasted. As soon as the fact that Jenna was back to normal sank in, the decision he'd made the night before had started preying on his mind. He was going to ask Jenna on a date, but first he would buy her a gift. Something special, too, not like the inexpensive, silly little presents they exchanged at Christmas and birthdays. Something that would let her know he was serious.

But what? Peter couldn't figure it out. He'd been obsessing for twenty-four hours, and he still had no idea.

"Look! Stop there!" Jenna cried suddenly, pointing up the road to the right-hand shoulder.

A roadside produce stand had come into view in a small, packed-dirt clearing. Built of raw, unpainted wood and blue plastic tarps, it was certainly nothing fancy. Out on the ground in front of it were several enormous pumpkins. A couple of cars had pulled over already, and two women inspected the farmer's wares while their preschool-age children hugged the pumpkins, patting them in apparent awe. Peter put on the brakes and pulled over, his tires churning up the gravel at the side of the road.

"Okay, remember," he told Jenna as the car came

to a stop. "We want to get the best possible price, so we need to ask about lower prices for higher quantities. If we can get a better deal by buying more pumpkins, we'll buy them and figure out how to sell them later."

"There's only three hundred and ninety-five dollars in the Eight Prime account. Plus Nicole's starter change. We can't go much past that."

"I have about eighty dollars in my savings account. It's not much, but we can use it if it helps. Eight Prime can pay me back later."

"I have almost two hundred dollars," Jenna offered. "We can use that, too."

Peter smiled, happy his friend was acting like herself again. "Well, between the three accounts, we ought to have plenty. But don't forget—we might find someone who'll give us some pumpkins for free. If we can find a few different people who are willing to donate, we might not have to buy anything."

Jenna's expression was excited as she reached for the car door handle. "This is going to be so fun!" She let herself out and hurried over to the pumpkins, crouching down beside them in her faded Levi's. Peter lingered behind in the car a moment, watching through the windshield.

When he looked at Jenna these days, part of him still saw the girl he'd met in sixth grade: funny, feisty, with hair down to her waist and perpetual scrapes from climbing to her backyard tree house. Most of him saw what everyone else did: a good-hearted teenager who could be trusted, someone to count on—his very best friend. But part of him saw Jenna now in a way that was quite new: as an increasingly pretty girl who would become a beautiful woman—one he wanted to spend his life with.

"Hey, Peter! Come on, slowpoke," Jenna called, waving him over. The afternoon sunlight played off the highlights in her brown hair, and her cheeks were pink with excitement and fall.

Peter got out of the car slowly, mesmerized. He wished he had a camera or some other way of freezing that one perfect moment forever.

"What are you doing? You look like you're going to be sick."

"Very funny," he said, walking toward her.

Jenna smiled, her cheeks compressing into perfect dimples, and Peter felt his heart flip over.

*Oh, man, Altmann,* he groaned to himself. *Are you ever in deep.*


"Wait!" Jenna said, her eyes on the stores up ahead. "Can you stop here a minute? I can buy a watch battery at that jeweler's."

"Sure." Peter slowed the car and parked it on the street.

Despite how tired she was from looking at pumpkins all afternoon, Jenna was eager to make this one last stop. Her wristwatch had quit sometime after the third farm, and it had been bugging her ever since. It was a stroke of luck that Peter had chosen to drive home right past the store where her parents had bought the watch.

They pushed through the glass door into the little shop, only to see the jeweler, Mr. Davin, walking toward them with a heavy ring of keys.

"Well, hello, Jenna," he said, stopping halfway to the door. "You got here in the nick of time—I was just about to lock up." He put the keys in a front pocket of his funny, old-fashioned apron. "How's that watch holding up?"

"Good. But it needs a battery." She stripped the stopped watch off her wrist and held it out to him. "I can come back, though, if—"

"Don't be silly," Mr. Davin interrupted. "That'll only take a minute. You kids wait out here, and I'll do this in back." The kindly old man wandered off, Jenna's watch clutched in one work-gnarled hand.

"I guess we might as well sit down," Peter said, sinking into a chair by the door. "It's amazing how tired you can get just driving around in the car."

"I know." But instead of sitting next to Peter, Jenna wandered restlessly around the shop, checking out the items in Mr. Davin's big glass cases.

Normally she wasn't particularly interested in jewelry. She usually wore her watch and a gold cross, but that was about it. Mr. Davin's shop was special, though. The old craftsman was famous throughout Missouri for his beautiful engagement sets and the huge selection of heart-shaped jewelry he designed and made himself. Every piece was unique, and Jenna found herself gradually entranced as she wandered from case to case.

*Wouldn't it be romantic to have a guy give me something like this?* she thought with a mental sigh. The next second, though, she knew she didn't mean just *any* guy—she meant Miguel del Rios. Her eyes skimmed over the gleaming items in the cases. *You'd know he really liked you then.*

She tried to imagine Miguel slipping one of Mr. Davin's heart-shaped rings on her finger or clasping the chain of a delicate diamond heart around her neck, but the image wouldn't come. Jenna scowled and increased her concentration. *Maybe if you pretend you're Leah,* she thought bitterly, stepping to the next case.

And that was where she saw it—the most perfect piece in the entire store: a promise bracelet of pure, polished gold. The top of the bracelet was made of a free-form open heart about half an inch across, while a rich, twisted gold chain completed the circle of the wrist, joining into each side of the heart with an intricate, hand-shaped clasp. Jenna stared, wishing it were hers. It wasn't just the bracelet's beauty that had seduced her, it was the symbolism: the way the two separate ends of the chain came together like two separate people—two different souls joined in a single perfect heart. She was so taken with it that she stood motionless in front of the case, imagining it on her wrist. Imagining Miguel putting it on her wrist . . .

"Which one are you looking at?" Peter asked suddenly over her shoulder.

Jenna jumped. "What? Oh. Nothing in particular."

"Come on, Jenna. I saw you over here practically drooling. Which one do you like?"

Jenna didn't want to tell him, but she wasn't sure why not. She finally shrugged and pointed to the bracelet. "That one." After all, it wasn't as if Peter knew she'd been thinking about Miguel. *Thank God,* she added silently, her heart skipping at the mere idea.

Peter bent to get a closer look as Mr. Davin shuffled back out with her watch. "All done!" he announced. "That'll be five dollars."

Jenna paid hurriedly and thanked the old man, then rushed out onto the sidewalk. The cool early-evening air soothed her hot, embarrassed cheeks and she breathed in deeply, trying to regain her composure.

She was a fool to have dreamed that Miguel del Rios would ever be interested in her. Why couldn't she just accept the fact that she'd never have a chance? That her little fantasy was over? Jenna shook her head angrily. Instead she was picking out jewelry.

"Hey, Jenna, what's the matter?" Peter asked, catching up with her on the sidewalk.

"Nothing. I just . . . it was hot in there."

One thing was for sure—she never wanted to see that bracelet again.

Nicole felt herself drifting as Pastor Ramsey rambled through his long sermon. She'd promised to pay attention in church from now on, but everything seemed to conspire against her. The hush over the congregation, the deep, sonorous voice of the pastor, and the hazy, rose-colored light through the stained glass windows all put her in a sleepy trance.

*Stay awake*, she commanded herself sternly, shaking her head and focusing on the open Bible in her lap. *You can do it*.

It was no use. A moment later, she was daydreaming again. It was her latest, favorite daydream too—the one about how devastated Jesse Jones was going to be when she won the modeling contest.

Nicole's eyes glazed over as the familiar fantasy played out in her head: first the tiara and roses, then her victory walk, then mass adoration, and finally—sweetest of all—the chance to rub Jesse's snobby, too-good nose in it.

Beside her, Nicole's parents rose unexpectedly to

their feet. Nicole scrambled to close her Bible and retrieve a hymnal from the pew as people began to sing. Luckily the hymn was one she knew. She let the hymnal slip back into its dusty wooden pocket and sang along with the others, the words coming automatically.

Nicole's father sang on her right, his bass voice more of a rumble than a melody. Her mother sang soprano on his other side, doing her best to sing out and sing well, putting way too much effort into it as far as Nicole was concerned. After all, singing well was what the choir was for. Anything too enthusiastic from the floor always felt like showing off to Nicole. Her mom was embarrassing her, and if Nicole had a prayer in her heart just then, it was that the hymn would end quickly so that she could slink down into her seat and hide.

She grimaced at the thought, instantly regretting her own shallowness. *Good one, Nicole.* Wasn't that exactly the type of self-centered behavior she was trying to outgrow? Who cared if her mother wanted to turn every hymn into Handel's *Messiah*? *Oh, perfect. Score two.* Nicole shook her head, discouraged. When she'd decided to change her life, she'd had no idea how hard it was going to be.

*It's all this thinking about the modeling contest,* she realized as the song came to an end and the members of the congregation took their seats at last.

*And about stupid Jesse Jones. You're getting off track again.*

If she was ever on track to begin with. For a few short hours when Kurt had died, everything had seemed so clear. The futility of the road she was on had been obvious, and in that moment she'd glimpsed the pointlessness of material things. But that vision was already fading. If she didn't keep her priorities in order, Nicole knew her new path would slip away too.

*Maybe I shouldn't enter the U.S. Girls contest after all.* But the thought was like a knife in her heart. How could she pass up the chance to be what she'd always dreamed—a real model? And how could modeling be bad for her, as long as she kept the important things in view?

*No, you'll be okay,* she reassured herself, feeling a little lightheaded from the racing of her pulse. *You know what you're doing now. You won't let the world turn your head again.*

The thought comforted her. *Besides*, she rationalized, *aren't I working my butt off with Eight Prime? That's got to be earning me points somewhere.*

Nicole smiled dreamily as once again her thoughts wandered off to the land of roses and tiaras. There was nothing in the Bible that said a girl couldn't have a little fun.

# Nine

"Now, that's *art!*" one of the basketball players at the back of Peter's third-period class yelled as Mr. McIntosh clicked the button and a slide of Botticelli's *Birth of Venus* filled the large projection screen.

Peter rolled his eyes skyward and wondered why Mr. McIntosh bothered. At least one guy in the room shouted that same thing every time the subject of the painting was nude and female, which happened frequently now that they were studying the Renaissance. Peter was as normal as the next guy, but he was starting to think it was possible to take art appreciation too far.

"Yes. Quite," Mr. McIntosh agreed, pretending not to catch the real meaning behind the comment. Then he launched into an impassioned lecture on the history and special features of the painting.

Peter only half listened as his teacher rattled on. He really liked the class, and Mr. McIntosh was one of the best teachers he'd ever had, but Peter had already studied *Birth of Venus*. It didn't take his full attention to jot down the few details he didn't already know. Instead his thoughts turned to the heart-shaped bracelet Jenna liked so well.

It wasn't the kind of gift Peter would have thought of on his own, but then again, he hadn't been able to figure out *what* to get her. And the bracelet was romantic, not to mention something he knew she really wanted. There *was* a problem, though: it cost more than two hundred dollars.

Ever since he could remember, Peter had been involved in one charity or another, and for the last two years, since he and Chris had started the Junior Explorers program, he'd barely had time for anything else. He was proud of what he'd accomplished—he'd do it again in a second—but all that volunteering had prevented him from holding a paying job. As a result, he had almost no money. He certainly didn't have two hundred dollars.

*There's nearly four hundred dollars in the Eight Prime account*, an unexpected little voice in his head piped up. *You could borrow some money and pay it back later.*

Peter shook his head emphatically, barely aware of his classmates anymore. It would be wrong to take money from Eight Prime. The group trusted him to keep it safe, and that was why they'd made him treasurer in the first place. Dipping into those funds would be a total betrayal of trust.

*Not if you pay it back,* the inner voice argued. *Pay it back with interest.*

But how? His parents gave him enough money to pay for gas, lunch, and the odd pizza or ice cream sundae, but his allowance didn't stretch much further than that; on the rare occasions when it did, Peter usually spent it on things for the Junior Explorers. The eighty dollars he'd managed to save was money he'd received as birthday gifts from distant relatives—and he wasn't due for a birthday anytime soon. He'd never be able to pay back Eight Prime.

*Of course you will. Eventually. It's not like we're buying the bus next week. You can start biking to school and making lunch at home and save up your allowance.*

It was true, Peter realized. But then he remembered something important: all the money in the Eight Prime account was going to be needed to buy the pumpkins.

*So you'll wait until after the sale. But after that there's nothing to stop you. A little loan—that's all you want. You can borrow it and pay it back and no one will ever know.*

The slide projector at the front of the room roused itself with a loud *whir-click.* Peter's attention snapped back to the screen as the light suddenly died, then flashed back out in mellowed colors.

Mr. McIntosh sighed reverently. "Just to compare, here's another version of Venus, from later on, in the sixteenth century. This is Titian's *Venus of Urbino.*"

"Now that's *art!*" declared a classmate.

Melanie was the last to arrive for the Eight Prime "pumpkin progress" meeting behind the cafeteria that Monday. The other members were already sitting in a circle on the grass, their lunches spread out in front of them. Melanie looked around, then quickly slipped in between Peter and Leah, as far from Jesse as she could get without sitting by Nicole. Quietly she opened her sack lunch and unwrapped a piece of cold pizza.

"There are two different farms I think would give us a good price," Peter was saying. "And we'll get at least some pumpkins donated. But before we do any final negotiating, we need to decide how many we think we can sell."

"Tell them about the church sale," Jenna urged from Peter's other side.

"Yeah, we need to talk about that, too." Peter looked around the circle. "I spoke to Reverend Thompson at our church yesterday. If we want to, he'll let us sell pumpkins in the church parking lot one Sunday after services. I think we'd get a good response, because our congregation knows all about the Junior Explorers."

Melanie saw Jesse glance her way in the pause that followed, as if he fully expected her to throw a big tantrum. In fact, everyone was looking at her—even Leah. The whole group apparently thought the same thing.

"I think it's a fine idea," Melanie said, directing a haughty look at Jesse. "Peter and I already discussed it in private."

Jesse's expression was so shocked that Melanie could barely keep the smirk off her face. She had a feeling it was going to keep Jesse awake at night trying to figure out when she'd done *anything* privately with Peter—and that was just fine with her.

"I think we ought to do it," Ben said. He was eating a tuna sandwich, apparently oblivious to the big glob of mayonnaise on his upper lip. "If your congregation already supports the Junior Explorers, selling them pumpkins ought to be easy."

Peter nodded. "I think we'll do well, and so do my parents."

"Mine too," Jenna chimed in. "They've already promised to buy us girls a pumpkin apiece."

Leah laughed. "That's a pretty good haul right there."

There was more discussion, but within a few minutes the group had agreed to hold two sales, one at school and another at Peter's church.

"That reminds me," Peter said, turning to Leah. "Did you talk to Principal Kelly yet? Is he going to let us use the quad?"

"I haven't had a chance," Leah apologized. "But I promise I'll do it soon."

"So how many pumpkins do you guys think we'll sell?" Miguel asked, turning to Jenna. "And what are they going to cost us?"

Jenna shook her head. "It's hard to say. I wouldn't be surprised if we sold a hundred at church, though."

"A *hundred*?" Melanie repeated, surprised. "Just how big is this church?"

"Probably nearly every family will buy at least one, and some will buy two or three," Peter said by way of explanation. "Look at the Conrads—they're buying five."

"I wonder if we can sell a hundred at school, too," Leah mused.

"At least!" Ben said enthusiastically. "We've got *fourteen* hundred students here."

"Yeah, but how many of them have any money?" Nicole asked skeptically. "Or will spend it on a pumpkin if they do? That's the kind of thing your parents buy."

"We need to play up the charity aspect," Melanie suggested. "People will buy them if they know they're helping little kids."

"Maybe," Nicole said grudgingly, and Melanie had to bite back a scathing retort. She wasn't sure whom she was more fed up with—Jesse for being such a jerk to Nicole, or Nicole for being such a

120

jerk to her. If Melanie had ever cared enough about Nicole's opinion to set her straight, she didn't anymore.

*Let her think that Jesse and I are the hottest thing on four legs,* Melanie thought vindictively. *I hope it drives her crazy!*

"I'll bet we can sell more like *two* hundred at school," Jesse said. "Especially if we get the sports teams on board. I'll bring in the football players if Miguel will talk to the water polo team."

"Sure," said Miguel. "I'll let 'em know."

"Well, then, are we willing to commit to three hundred—or as close to that number as we can afford?" Peter asked, looking around. Everybody nodded. "Okay. I'll start making some calls."

"When are we going to hold the sales?" Melanie asked.

Peter looked uncertain. "Well, first we need to make sure we have the pumpkins. And Leah still needs to talk to the principal. I don't think we're in a big hurry, though. It might be better to wait until mid-October."

"We shouldn't wait *too* long," Ben cautioned. Melanie noticed that he'd finally wiped the goo off his face. "Otherwise everyone will have already bought one."

"Right. Well, I guess we don't need to have another meeting this week," Peter said. "Let's get together again after I talk to the farmers."

Everyone said that was fine and began finishing their lunches, but Melanie couldn't stay. She needed to find Vanessa and make sure the squad leader hadn't called another last-minute practice after school. The new stunt was coming along, but they were still a long way from being ready to perform it at Friday's game.

"Well, got to fly," she said, stuffing her half-eaten pizza back into her lunch bag and rising from the grass. "Duty calls." She brushed off the seat of her pants, waved good-bye, then turned and walked away.

*I don't know what's worse,* she thought unhappily as she hurried off to find the other cheerleaders, *lunch with Jesse, or lunch with Vanessa!*

*I can't believe I forgot to write that stupid English paper,* Jenna thought with a groan as she climbed the stairs to her bedroom. She'd had all weekend to work on Mr. Smythe's touchy-feely assignment, but somehow it had slipped her mind. Now she was going to have to crank it out at the last minute, along with the rest of today's homework. She'd be lucky if she got to sleep before midnight.

She opened her bedroom door and shuddered at the sight of the Clue posters still plastered to the walls on Maggie's side. *At least Maggie isn't here,* she consoled herself, wondering how long her younger sister would be gone. She dropped her backpack onto her bed and sat down cross-legged beside it, emptying out the bag's contents and dividing things into piles. *I guess I should just enjoy her absence for as long as it lasts.*

Jenna had geometry homework, as usual, in addition to the paper for Mr. Smythe. She also had to memorize the lyrics for two new songs, write up the results of the biology experiment she'd done in class that day, and draw a design for a weaving project in textiles. *I even have homework in the classes that are supposed to be fun!* she thought, feeling slightly overwhelmed. She shuffled the piles around in front of her, trying to decide where to start.

*Okay, first Mr. Smythe,* she decided, sticking out her tongue. *I might as well get that out of the way. Then I'll do the biology and the weaving design, and I'll save the geometry until after dinner.* Jenna picked up a spiral pad and flipped to a blank page. Then she uncapped a pen and prepared to write what was probably the stupidest assignment in the history of the English-speaking world.

Nothing came to her. Not a word.

"Oh, come on," she muttered. "You've got strong feelings like crazy. Just pick one and write something."

She stared intently at the lined white sheet in front of her, awaiting inspiration, but the paper stared right back, as stubbornly blank as before.

Jenna could feel her mind going as blank as the paper.

"*Noooo*," she groaned. "I don't have time for writer's block today!" It was on its way, though—Jenna recognized the signs. If she didn't get something down fast, she was going to be in big trouble.

"Love!" she announced, writing the word at the top of the page. And then she started scribbling underneath it as fast as she possibly could.

> Of all the emotions a person can feel, I think love is the strongest. And I don't mean the kind of love you feel for a friend, or a sister, or even your parents. I'm talking about <u>true</u> love. The kind of gut-wrenching, palm-sweating, turns-you-inside out love you only feel for that one special person.

Jenna had no idea if what she'd just written was good, bad, or awful, but at least she was getting

some words down on paper. She charged ahead
without reading what she'd done.

Love is the best emotion
there is, but it's also the
cruelest. If the other person
doesn't love you back, it
feels like your life is over.
Not only that, but you feel
_so_ stupid!

I thought I was in love
with this guy named Miguel
for two whole years. I day-
dreamed about him all the
time, and I looked for him
wherever I went. When I finally
met him this year, I was so
excited. But before I even got
to know him, I found out
he liked someone else. The
worst part is, now I have

*to do things with him.
and his new girlfriend
all the time.*

*I feel like a total idiot.
And since I found out, I'm
not even sure I know what
love is. Sure, I understand
the kind of love a person
feels for her friends, or sisters,
or parents. But what about
true love? What about the
kind of love Dana Fraser
and Kurt Englbehrt had? Will
I ever know what that feels
like?*

Jenna stopped to rest a minute, the danger of a writer's block behind her. Her lips moved slightly as her eyes skimmed two pages filled with purple ink.

"I can't turn this in!" she moaned. "Anyone who sees it will know it's about Miguel del Rios. If Mr.

Smythe ever leaked it, I'd be the laughingstock of the entire school."

And Mr. Smythe was exactly the kind of person who *would* leak it, too. Knowing him, he'd probably read it aloud to the class and correct her grammar at the same time. *Today, people,* she could almost hear him saying, *we're going to ruin Ms. Conrad's life and learn to spot a sentence fragment while we're at it.*

Jenna jumped hurriedly off the bed, crumpled up the offending pages, and threw them into the wastebasket by her desk. The moment they hit the dented metal can, though, she knew she could never leave them there. What if someone emptied the trash and found them? What if *Maggie* found them? With a sharp intake of breath, Jenna snatched the crumpled sheets back out of the trash, glancing around for a safer place to put them. She smoothed the pages out on her desktop and folded them in half; then she opened the bottom drawer of her small desk and hid the essay at the very back, behind a boxed set of stationery and under a pad of graph paper. *There!* she thought with a sigh of relief. *No one will ever look for anything there, and I'll find a safe place to get rid of it later. Maybe the next time we have a fire in the fireplace . . .*

Her heart rate nearly back to normal, Jenna flopped down on her bed to try again with another subject—a subject safe for Mr. Smythe. This time she barely had to think at all. Her topic came to her in a flash. All that fooling around just to hide two sheets of paper had shown her the perfect subject for her next essay: Maggie.

"Frustration!" she said happily, writing it at the top of a clean page.

> *If you've never shared a room with a younger sister, then you've never truly experienced frustration.*

From there it was a breeze. There was Maggie's slovenliness, her love of stupid bands and their ugly posters, her immature little games, and last, but certainly not least, the complete and absolute lack of privacy that having her around entailed. Jenna filled up the pages so fast she lost count. She was finishing her last sentence when the antihero of her essay came crashing into the room.

"Whatcha doing?" Maggie asked.

"Nothing." Jenna slammed her steno pad shut.

"Oooh . . . Jenna's got a secret," Maggie chanted. She flopped onto her bed and lay there grinning, obviously hoping to be let in on it.

"I do not. It's just homework."

"That's Jenna—Little Miss Studious," Maggie teased, seeming to think her remark very clever.

"Do you have something you could be doing besides annoying me? I have too much work to do today to waste time talking to you."

Maggie sat up, offended. "Well, excuse me! What are *you* in such a bad mood for?"

"I'm not in a bad mood, all right? I'd just like a little peace and quiet."

"I know what your problem is. You're still bent out of shape because Mom got you in trouble. That was your own fault, Jenna! I didn't tell her anything—she came in here and found those sheets herself."

Jenna's only reply was a lingering, disgusted glance at the Clue posters on Maggie's side of the room.

Maggie pressed on, undeterred. "I think you're just jealous because I have a date on Friday and you don't."

"You couldn't pay me to go to that hokey little junior-high-school dance," Jenna fired back disdainfully.

"It's the *Fall Fantasy*!" Maggie returned, outraged. "You're just mad because I'm going with Scott, and Mom bought *me* a new dress, and you never go anywhere with anyone but Peter—"

"Give me a break!" Jenna cried, blood rushing to her cheeks. "Do you really think I care in the slightest? Like I'm really jealous of your dorky little boyfriend or that *hideous* dress you picked out! I

129

wouldn't wear that dress with a bag over my head!" There was no way she'd ever admit it, but Maggie's shot had hit home.

"You take that back!" Maggie demanded. But there was a quiver in her voice, and Jenna knew she'd finally gotten the better of the little pain in the rear.

A triumphant surge of adrenaline made Jenna smile as she gathered up her homework. "I don't think so," she said condescendingly.

She sailed out of the room to type her paper on the computer in the den, on top of the situation with Maggie at last.

Victory. *That* strong feeling was sweeter than Jenna could have imagined.

# Ten

"Hi, Nicole. Hi, Courtney. Is it okay if I join you?"

Nicole turned her head to see Jenna walking up to their bench at the edge of the quad. The period was already more than half over, but Jenna held what appeared to be a full, unopened lunch sack in her hand.

"Uh, sure. Go ahead," Nicole said, surprised, She scooted closer to Courtney to make room for Jenna, who plopped down on her other side. Courtney drew in a loud, pained breath, but Nicole gave her friend a warning elbow in the ribs.

"Thanks a lot," Jenna said, oblivious to Courtney's displeasure as she opened her brown paper bag. "I told Peter I had to study during lunch, but I finished early and now I don't know where he is."

She pulled a sandwich out of a Baggie and started eating as if famished. The smell of salami reaching Nicole's nose drove her almost crazy with hunger. It had been bad enough to sit and starve through Courtney's lunch without repeating the process with Jenna.

"So, what were you studying?" Nicole asked to distract herself from the growling in her stomach.

"We had to memorize two new songs for choir. I had so much other homework last night that I didn't get around to it."

"Oh." Nicole's eyes were so glued to Jenna's thick homemade sandwich that she barely heard.

"Do you want a bite?" Jenna offered suddenly. "I'll split it with you."

"No! Uh, no thanks," Nicole said hastily, embarrassed to have been so obvious. "I already ate."

"She did not," Courtney contradicted her. "Nicole doesn't eat anymore."

Nicole knew her friend was paying her back for making her sit with a member of the God Squad. She shot her an annoyed glance before turning back to Jenna. "I'm kind of on a diet," she admitted.

"You? You're so thin!" Jenna exclaimed. "What do you need to diet for?"

Nicole beamed and was about to thank Jenna for the compliment when Leah stepped out of the crowd.

"Hi, you guys. Am I missing a reunion or something?"

"No, just me wolfing down my lunch before class," said Jenna. "Where's Miguel?"

Leah seemed taken aback. "I don't know. Why would I?"

Jenna shrugged and returned to her sandwich.

"Sit down," Courtney invited, scrunching over to make a place for Leah at her end of the bench. "Nicole was just telling us about her anorexia."

"I am *not* anorexic!" Nicole protested. "Geez, Courtney. I'm just on a diet."

"I thought you'd been losing weight," Leah said, turning sideways on the bench. "You're thin enough now, though, aren't you?"

"I thought you were thin enough before!" Jenna said.

Nicole drank in their praise, thrilled that someone had finally noticed. Of course, Jenna's opinion wasn't too reliable, since she needed to lose a few pounds herself. But Leah was extremely thin— willowy even—and her opinion mattered.

"I'm getting there," Nicole said, feeling unexpectedly shy from all the attention. "I still have a little more to go, though."

Leah raised her eyebrows. "I think you're there," she said firmly. "You don't need to lose more weight."

"Well . . . thanks," Nicole muttered bashfully, her cheeks on fire. "But they say the camera adds ten pounds, so models actually need to be underweight to look good in pictures."

"You're a model?" Jenna asked, her eyes widening.

Courtney snorted. "Every night from midnight until two A.M.—or whenever it is she dreams."

"Funny, Courtney," Nicole shot back, stung. "For

your information, I've decided to compete in that U.S. Girls contest."

"You're kidding! I thought I talked you out of that!"

"Not arguing with someone isn't the same as agreeing with them," Nicole retorted hotly. "Believe it or not, I don't do everything you say."

Courtney seemed about to deliver a crushing comeback when Leah intervened. "What's the U.S. Girls contest?" she asked.

Nicole took a deep, calming breath, then launched into an impassioned explanation of the store, its new line of jeans, and how she'd be going to St. Louis to compete in the Missouri portion of the contest.

"Wow!" said Jenna. "It sounds exciting."

"Did your parents say you could drive to St. Louis?" Courtney asked at the exact same time.

Nicole ignored Courtney and turned toward Jenna. "It *is* going to be exciting. You ought to come." The invitation was out of her mouth before she knew it was coming, but when Nicole saw Jenna's eyes light up, she didn't regret it a bit.

"You mean, go with you?" Jenna asked excitedly. "Oh, that would be so fun! Peter *never* wants to do things like that."

"I can't imagine why not," Courtney said dryly.

"We *all* ought to go," Leah suggested. "Let's invite Melanie, too, and make a day of it."

"What a good idea!" Courtney agreed quickly,

shooting Nicole a triumphant look. "That would be great."

Nicole could have kicked her friend in the shin for agreeing to such a horrible plan. She knew she was just paying her back for contradicting her.

"Well, *we* can all go. But I, uh, don't think there's going to be room in the car for Melanie," Nicole lied. The last thing she needed was to have her big moment overshadowed by that relentlessly perfect cheerleader from hell. "Not unless *you* want to stay home, Court," she added pointedly.

Courtney laughed, a devious glint in her bottle green eyes. "Are you kidding? I wouldn't miss this trip for anything."

Leah rounded the last bookcase at the very back of the CCHS library and smiled at the sight that met her eyes. "Hi," she said breathlessly.

"Hi," Miguel whispered back.

The two of them were alone at their new favorite place on campus—a study table so far behind the book stacks that most people didn't even know about it, let alone venture back there.

"What homework have you got today?" Leah asked, slipping into the seat beside him. They turned their faces toward the wall for extra privacy.

Miguel shrugged. "Just a bunch of garbage. The usual. If you want, I'm willing to blow it all off and take you to the lake." He was so clearly doing his best to make a noble, self-sacrificing expression that Leah had to stifle a giggle.

"You'd like that, wouldn't you?" she teased.

"Yeah. I would." Miguel glanced quickly over his shoulder to make sure no one was around, then bent to kiss her.

Leah felt an electric jolt as their lips came together, and the very real possibility that someone might catch them only added to the thrill. Her eyes closed instinctively and her heart fluttered faster. Her senses shut down one by one until she felt as if she were floating.

Miguel chuckled quietly, bringing her back to Earth. "It looks like *you'd* like it too."

Leah opened her eyes and worked to erase the canary-eating grin on her face. "You'll never know," she said, trying to sound mysterious. "Because *I'm* going to do *my* homework."

She pulled her biology text out of the pile of books in front of her and flipped it open quickly, before she could change her mind. Ms. Walker had assigned a chapter of reading, as well as the study questions at the end of the unit. "I know you at *least* have biology homework," Leah told Miguel, who still hadn't lifted a finger. "If I do, you do."

Miguel shrugged and looked up toward the dingy ceiling. "Pea genetics. I'm not sure I'll survive the thrill."

Leah shook her head. "I know studying the genetics of pea plants doesn't seem very exciting *now*—"

"To say the least."

"But it really *is* important. I mean, can you believe that when Darwin came up with evolution, he knew literally nothing about genetics? Isn't that amazing?"

Miguel smiled, his eyes focused on her lips. "I think we have different versions of amazing."

"Well, then," Leah said, determined to ignore the hint. "How about the fact that Mendel was a priest? You have to admit that's kind of interesting."

"Who's Mendel?" Miguel asked absently.

"Miguel! Mendel's the pea plant guy!"

"Oh, right. And *why* is his religion interesting again?"

"I just think it's interesting that he had one. I mean, now it seems like everyone expects you to believe in either science *or* religion, but historically lots of scientists were clergymen."

Miguel shrugged. "Only because the clergy were educated."

"Yeah, but that's not the only reason. People didn't use to see a contradiction between God and science. Everyone was so convinced that God created everything directly, it never even occurred to them that science could discover anything different. What a crisis it must have been when Darwin proposed evolution!"

"Here we go with evolution again . . . ," Miguel groaned, heaving a fake sigh.

Leah laughed. "You know you love it."

"For your information," said Miguel, looking quite pleased with himself, "even the Pope accepts evolution."

"Yeah, *this* one does," Leah countered.

But Miguel was undeterred. "If evolution happens, it doesn't mean God doesn't exist. A lot of people think he *used* evolution to create man— that it was all part of his plan."

Leah smiled. Miguel had been studying up. "I know."

"And anyway, they still haven't been able to figure out how all those chemicals made the first living cell."

"I *know*. Isn't it fascinating?"

Miguel made a face. "More fascinating than pea plants."

"It's all related," Leah said, pushing his textbook toward him.

They finally settled down to study, but Leah's imagination was so fired up, she couldn't concentrate. When she'd met him, just a few weeks before, Miguel had refused to even discuss religion. Now they were debating it. Whether old wounds were finally healing or he was only making the effort to please her, Leah didn't know. Either way it was exciting.

"Hey, Miguel," she whispered, interrupting his reading.

He looked up from his biology assignment as if happy to be disturbed. The smile on his lips reached all the way into his eyes. "Yeah?"

She had intended to ask him to brunch with her parents that weekend, but the way he was smiling at her knocked the idea right out of her head.

*I'll ask him tomorrow,* she decided, leaning over to kiss him. A few minutes later she couldn't have told him what brunch even was.

Peter stood on the pavement outside Anthony Hall, unable to believe the chaos all around him. It was almost nine o'clock on a Tuesday night, but the place looked like Party Central. Students were hanging out the windows of the five-story building, carrying on shouted conversations with students on the ground, and music blared from four or five different sources. The different tunes blended and clashed as the echoes bounced off the nearby buildings. Meanwhile, around the base of the residence hall, skateboarders and Rollerbladers were trying out new stunts and competing in what could only be speed trials.

"So this is dorm life," Peter muttered, stunned. He didn't know now what he'd expected, but he'd kind of thought it would have more to do with frantic studying and drinking too much coffee. He rechecked the scribbled notes on the scrap of paper in his hand, then began walking toward the cube-shaped brick building in front of him.

It was easy to find the stairwell Chris had described on the telephone. Peter slipped into it gratefully, feeling slightly less conspicuous in its shelter. He was sure everyone who even glanced his way knew he was a high-school kid, and he hated looking lost. He checked his notes again. *Room 329—third floor.*

Chris answered immediately when Peter knocked. "Peter! You made it, man," he said, throwing the door open wide and motioning Peter inside. "Did you have any trouble finding it?"

"Uh, not really," Peter said, looking around the tiny space. The room was a perfect square, about ten feet on each wall, and into that insignificant area were crammed two single beds, two built-in desks with bookshelves, two little cupboards that Peter guessed were closets, a beat-up garage-sale table with a computer on top and a stereo underneath, and all the clothes, books, shoes, sports equipment, and assorted junk two college guys needed to get through the day. Chris's roommate was sitting on the unmade bed by the window. Peter suddenly noticed there were no chairs in the room except for two very uncomfortable-looking metal ones wedged in under the desks.

"Welcome to my humble abode," Chris joked,

gesturing vaguely toward the mess. "Hey, Keith, this is my friend, Peter Altmann. Peter, meet Keith Logan."

Keith nodded affably. "How's it going, man?"

"Fine, thanks." Peter's eyes still roamed the room distractedly. "How do you guys *live* here?" he blurted out a second later. "I've seen *hamsters* in bigger cages."

Chris laughed. "You're not impressed by the palatial facilities here Chez Anthony?"

"I think I'm getting claustrophobic."

"You get used to it," Keith said, rising from his bed. "But it takes a few days. Kind of like living on a ship or something, I guess. I'm going down to the Coffee Cavern," he told Chris, grabbing a coat and backpack off a hook on the wall. "Be back in a couple of hours."

"Okay. See ya."

Chris's roommate had to sidestep around Chris and Peter just to get to the doorway. "Nice meeting you," Peter called as Keith reached freedom and pulled the door closed behind him.

Chris grabbed one of the metal desk chairs and dragged it out into a tiny area of open floor. "Have a seat," he offered, dropping onto the edge of his bed. "If you don't stay too long, your butt might not fall asleep."

Peter sat down on the hard folding chair, marveling at Chris's cheerfulness. He didn't *think* he was spoiled, but he also didn't think he'd adjust to dorm life as happily as his friend had. "You like it here, don't you?" he asked, trying not to sound amazed.

Chris shrugged. "Yeah. Why not? It's a little crowded, but, like Keith said, you get used to that. And the good part is that it's really convenient. You meet a lot of people. Besides . . ." A shadow passed over Chris's face. "Anything's better than living at home."

Peter nodded, finally understanding. Chris rarely spoke about his family, or the tough years before he'd met Maura.

"But, hey, enough about me," Chris added hurriedly, scooting to the edge of the bed and sitting up straighter. "I'm dying to know what was important enough to finally bring you out here. That story you told me was full of more noninformation than a government press release."

Peter smiled apologetically. "I didn't want to talk about it on the phone."

"No kidding! You're CIA material, Altmann, I'm telling you."

Chris's grin was infectious, and Peter smiled too, in spite of the fact that he found the situation a little embarrassing.

"I just . . . well . . . this is *big*, Chris. Really big. And I don't want anyone else to know yet. I've got to talk to someone, though, and I knew you'd understand."

Chris's expression turned serious. "Are you in trouble, Peter?"

"No! No," Peter assured him quickly. "I . . . I'm in love."

"In love!" Chris hooted. "Congratulations, man! Who is it? No, wait! Let me guess." He rubbed a hand back and forth through his spiky brown flat-top. "Wow . . . I don't know . . . when do you even have *time* to meet girls? It must be somebody at school. It's someone at your high school, right?"

Peter opened his mouth, but before he could say a word Chris jumped to his feet. "It's *Melanie*! It's that Melanie Andrews, isn't it? Altmann, you *dog*! Way to go!"

Chris reached to high-five him, but Peter shook his head. "No. It's Jenna," he said quietly.

Chris froze, shocked. Then he lowered his un-slapped hands and stared. "Jenna," he said at last, dropping back onto his bed. "Wow. I had no idea."

"Neither does she," Peter said miserably. "I haven't got up the nerve to tell her yet."

"But she must suspect, don't you think? You two spend so much time together . . . she must have *some* idea."

"Do you think so?" Peter asked hopefully. "It doesn't seem that way to me."

"No?" Chris's surprise was becoming confusion.

"Then—no offense, bud—but why are you here telling me and not her?"

"I don't know *how* to tell her," Peter said. "That's why I came here tonight. I was hoping you could help me out."

"*Me?*" Chris protested. "What do you want *me* to do?"

"Well . . . you have a girlfriend. How did you tell Maura when you decided you loved her?"

Chris laughed. "Peter, man, I knew I loved Maura the first second I saw her. I didn't *have* to tell her—she could read it all over my face."

"You're lucky she didn't slap you, then," Peter muttered. When Chris and Maura had met in high school, Chris was into using drugs and hanging out, and Maura was the sheltered youngest daughter of a Sunday-school teacher.

"You're not lying," Chris agreed, not in the least offended. "Anyway, my point is that things with you and Jenna are totally different. You're already friends, for one thing. She can bring you home to her parents, for another . . ." Chris made a face, his thoughts clearly wandering back to his own situation.

Peter knew Chris had given up drinking, drugs, *and* cigarettes, dropped most of his old friends, and started going to Bible study to win Maura over. A year later, he'd been baptized. But Mr. Kennedy didn't believe Chris was serious—about his faith *or* about Maura. It was taking much, much longer to woo Mr. Kennedy than it had to convince his tender-hearted daughter.

"I think you ought to just tell her," Chris concluded, coming back to Peter's problem. "What have you got to lose?"

"Only everything! What if the idea of me as a boyfriend totally repulses her? Maybe she won't even want to be friends anymore."

Chris shook his head impatiently. "Give yourself a little credit, man."

"Well," Peter said, taking a deep breath, "I'm going to tell her. But I want it to be special. I'm going to ask her out, and I'm going to give her a present, too."

"Not necessary," Chris opined, "but not a bad touch. What are you going to give her?"

Peter groaned. "That's *another* problem. I know she wants a bracelet in this store downtown, but it costs over two hundred dollars."

"Two hundred! That's too much."

"I don't know, It's really nice. . . ."

"It had *better* be—but that's not what I meant. I meant it's too much to spend on a first gift. I didn't even know you had that kind of money."

"I don't," Peter admitted glumly. "Actually, I was thinking about borrowing it from the Eight Prime account."

"You're taking the bus money?" Chris's eyes were wide with disbelief.

"I'd pay it back!"

"Yeah, well . . ." Chris didn't look convinced. "What does everyone else say?"

"Who?"

"The rest of Eight Prime. You're not going to take it without asking them, are you?"

"Do you think that would be wrong?"

"Duh! You know it would."

"Yeah," Peter acknowledged, totally defeated. He hadn't really expected Chris to say anything different, but there was no way he could tell Eight Prime why he wanted the money. It suddenly seemed he'd driven all the way out to the university for nothing. Well, not exactly *nothing*, he supposed. At least he'd gotten some moral support.

"So do you really think I have a chance with Jenna?" Peter asked. "I mean, even without the bracelet?"

"Of course," Chris said, clearly happy to be back on safer ground. "Think about it, Peter. You know she likes you as a friend. Plus she's never dated anyone the entire time I've known you guys. Now that I'm thinking about it, she probably feels the exact same way."

Peter's heart beat faster. It was true. Jenna *didn't* go on dates.

"And I'll tell you something else," Chris added.

"Jenna isn't the type of girl who'd be swayed by jewelry one way or the other. That's not how she was raised."

"You're right. I know," Peter agreed. "I just . . . I guess I wanted to do something kind of spectacular." He hesitated, then the rest of the truth came tumbling out. "Besides, I thought if she wore the bracelet then everyone would know. That she and I were together, I mean."

"Uh-huh. I know how *that* feels," Chris said, grinning wryly. "I tried to get a promise ring on Maura's finger for two whole years, but her dad kept making her give it back. I was in and out of that jeweler's shop more often than the armored truck."

"She wears one now," Peter pointed out.

"And every time I see it on her finger, I feel like the luckiest guy on earth. But the ring's not what it's about—not really. It's the *promise* that makes the difference."

"True." Peter rose slowly to his feet. "You know, I'm glad I came over here, Chris."

"Yeah?" Chris's brown eyes sparkled with mischief. "Then get ready to be *thrilled*."

"What are you talking about?"

"If you want, I'll lend you the two hundred bucks."

# Eleven

"Is everybody ready?" Melanie called anxiously, steeling herself for her last attempt of the day. "Here I come!" She started running.

"Just do it already," Tiffany grumbled as Melanie's feet hit the trampoline.

And then she was flying through the air, her hair whipping out behind her. The flip Melanie executed at the top of her arc was tight and precise, and she landed on the pyramid perfectly—her feet on target, her weight balanced evenly, and her arms overhead in a triumphant V.

"Beautiful!" Tanya cried. "That was the best one yet!"

"Way to go!" Lou Anne added. "Wow, that looked so cool, you guys."

Melanie leapt gracefully down to the mats on the gymnasium floor, where Tanya and Lou Anne each caught a hand to steady her. The other cheerleaders broke down the rest of the pyramid with practiced flair.

"I'm going to ask my dad to videotape us at the

game on Friday so I'll finally be able to see it," Angela said when everyone was on their feet.

Once again, Melanie realized that the only girls who could actually see her flip were Tanya and Lou Anne. *It must be so boring for everyone in the pyramid*, she thought, feeling slightly guilty. *Still, it wasn't my idea.* Melanie snuck a quick peek at Vanessa. Because of her height, the cheerleading captain had a bottom-row position—the most boring spot of all. *I wonder why she even wanted to do this?*

"Yeah, well, that's all for today," Vanessa said. Melanie couldn't tell if she was happy that they'd finally mastered the stunt or not. "I'm not calling a practice tomorrow. Rest up for the game on Friday."

"Hoo-*ray*!" Tiffany said, her tone making her opinion of Vanessa's extra practices clear.

"Vanessa!" Melanie protested. "I think we need the extra day! We're not going to get to practice before the game, and I've only landed this thing clean three times. I don't want to run out in front of the whole school on Friday night and do it cold."

"You're going to be doing it cold whether we practice tomorrow or not," Vanessa pointed out. "And there's nothing to gain by overpracticing—you've got it down, and everyone else needs a break."

"Hear, hear," Tiffany agreed. Before Vanessa could change her mind, Tiffany grabbed her gym bag and hurried toward the door. "See you all tomorrow," she called as she stepped out into the twilight.

"What time is it?" Melanie gasped. The sky showing through the crack of the closing door was the deep gray-blue of approaching nightfall. "It's almost dark!" She looked toward the caged clock at the end of the gym. "The clock says it's four-fifteen!"

"That clock's broken," Tanya told her. "It's been skipping back and forth all afternoon."

"I'm going to miss the last bus!" Melanie gathered her things in a panic, stuffed them into her gym bag, and raced for the door, any further discussion of a Thursday practice completely forgotten. Outside, the air was chilly, but Melanie barely noticed as she sprinted across campus toward the bus stop, her gym bag pounding her right thigh. *You didn't even wait to find out what time it really is*, she realized as she hit the long final stretch across CCHS's front lawn. *The bus could already be gone.* The little bus shelter was coming into view in the growing darkness up ahead, but Melanie couldn't tell whether anyone was in it. A wicked cramp burned in her side, bending her nearly double as she staggered the final few steps across the grass and rounded the end wall of the enclosure. All three benches inside were empty. The place was utterly deserted.

*You're so stupid!* she raged at herself. *You should have found out what time it was before you ran all the way over here. You should have caught a ride with one of the other girls.* She set her gym bag down on the end of the nearest bench and struggled to catch her breath.

*Okay. It's not the end of the world,* she thought, trying to calm down. *If you hurry back to the gym, maybe you can still catch someone. Football practice probably just let out. If the girls are already gone, maybe one of the players will drive you.*

The student parking lot wasn't that far away, but the cheerleaders were allowed to park in the special-events lot next to the gym when they had late practices. Melanie was sure all the girls who had cars would have moved them there, and that was where the players would be parked too. She groaned aloud at the thought of running back over the ground she'd just covered. The long afternoon of cheering practice and her impromptu cross-country sprint had left her bone tired. Meanwhile, it was getting darker by the minute. *If you don't get a ride with Tanya or someone, you're going to have to call Dad to come get you,* she reminded herself. *And he's probably half crocked by now.*

Reluctantly she picked up her bag and started trotting back toward the gym, every step increasing the agony in her side. She was barely halfway across the front lawn when Jesse's voice rang out.

"Hey, Melanie! Need a ride?"

She was so glad to hear those words at that

particular moment that she almost forgot what a low form of scum Jesse was and how seriously he revolted her. And though her anger returned a second later, she knew she couldn't refuse his offer. What if everyone else was already gone when she got back to the gym? Gritting her teeth, she smiled and waved to Jesse, who, for whatever reason, had left his car parked in the student parking lot.

By the time she reached the asphalt, Jesse had driven over to the edge, just to save her a few feet of walking. Melanie sank into the black leather passenger seat without a word, barely glancing at her chauffeur before fixing her gaze straight ahead through the windshield. To her amazement, Jesse didn't take advantage of the situation by giving her the third degree. Instead, he pulled into the thinning evening traffic and turned toward her house without a single question.

They rode in silence, the headlights of the oncoming cars white streaks in the gathering darkness. Melanie knew she ought to thank him, but she was still so annoyed with him she couldn't say anything nice. *If he wants to talk, let him start it,* she thought. But he didn't. For the first time since she'd met him, Jesse seemed fresh out of snappy comments.

By the time the BMW finally rolled to a stop in Melanie's driveway, the silence had become oppressive. Melanie jerked her door open and climbed out into the night, hesitating only a second to see if Jesse was going to say something.

"Well, thanks," she murmured when he remained silent. She began to push the door shut.

"Wait."

Melanie grimaced in the darkness. "What?"

"I swear I don't know why you're mad at me, Melanie. If you won't tell me what I did, how can I make it better?"

"You know what you did."

"No, I don't."

He had to be lying, but Melanie barely cared anymore. "Whatever. I've got to go."

She shut the car door, then turned her back on him and hurried up the walkway to her house. The massive front door was unlocked. She pushed it open a crack, slipped inside, and closed it quickly behind her, leaning against the smooth wood. No lamps were on in the two-story entry hall, but the backyard landscape lighting spilled through the bank of sliding glass doors at the perimeter of the formal living room, creeping as far as the polished marble under Melanie's feet and illuminating it in a cool gray glow. Melanie waited until she heard Jesse's car pull out of the driveway and drive off down the Andrewses' private road. Then she dropped her gym bag with a sigh and headed toward the kitchen.

*I wonder where I'll find Dad tonight*, she thought as

she opened the refrigerator door. *Poolhouse or den?* The carton of cottage cheese she'd eaten half of for breakfast was right where she'd left it . . . untouched. In fact, the only thing that seemed different in that enormous stainless-steel refrigerator was a noticeable decrease in the amount of beer. *Time for Dad to send Mrs. Murphy to the store again,* she thought, wondering what the part-time housekeeper's schedule was that week. *If it weren't for her and the pool guy and the gardener, nothing would ever get done around here.*

With a sigh, Melanie retrieved the cottage cheese and slammed the heavy door. Her dad always kept cash around for her to call for takeout, but that night it didn't seem worth the trouble. Instead, Melanie dug through a nearby drawer for a spoon and wandered toward the den.

*Ooh! First try,* she thought sarcastically. Her father was passed out on the couch. A blanket half covered his skinny white legs, and his ratty plaid bathrobe gaped open at the chest, showing how bony that too had become. He snored obliviously in a position that would have been impossible had he been sober, his open-mouthed profile lit by the rising and falling glow of the muted television set.

"More quality time with the family," Melanie muttered, reaching for the remote. She switched off the TV, then felt her way back down the dark hall to the dim entryway.

Her mother's paintings still dominated the entry walls, in the exact same places she and Jesse had hung them two weeks before, but they were already losing their power. The strange, almost intoxicating effect they'd had on her when she'd first rescued them from the storeroom had all but dissipated. And her father—the man who'd been moved to tears at the sight—no longer seemed to notice them at all. They had already faded into the grayness of his landscape, just like his ambition, his health, and Melanie herself.

Melanie flipped on a light switch and watched the paintings explode into color. Nothing. She stood there a long time, seeing but not feeling, a little carbon copy of her father.

She didn't even remember anymore what she'd thought hanging them up would accomplish.

"Is this for someone special?" Mr. Davin asked as he lifted Peter's selection out of the heavy plateglass case. The jeweler chuckled and shook his shaggy head. "What am I saying? They're *always* for someone special."

Peter smiled self-consciously and hoped the old man wouldn't figure out it was for Jenna—at least not until she was wearing it.

"How about some gift wrap?" the jeweler offered. "I have a pretty pink one the young ladies love." He winked at Peter. "No extra charge."

"That sounds great," Peter said, and Mr. Davin headed toward the back room.

Peter paced anxiously while he waited for the jeweler to reappear. He couldn't have said why he was suddenly so nervous. After all, Chris's pep talk the night before had done him a lot of good, and the bracelet was a no-brainer—he already knew she liked it.

*I'm not nervous, I'm excited*, he decided. *There's nothing wrong with that.*

"I used the pink ribbon, too. What do you think?" Mr. Davin asked loudly, startling Peter into whirling around. "Oops. Did I sneak up on you?"

"No. Uh, I mean, that's okay."

Then Peter saw the carefully wrapped package in the old man's hands. It was smaller than he had expected—Mr. Davin must have coiled the bracelet up and put it in a container about the size of a ring box. A smile spread over Peter's face at the sight of the deep pink paper with its creamy, barely pink ribbon and tiny, star-shaped bow. The whole package gave the impression of a perfect miniature—the biggest box under the Christmas tree, shrunk down to dollhouse size. Jenna was going to love it!

Peter could hardly wait to see the look on her face when he surprised her with it that weekend.

"Stop thinking about it," Jenna ordered herself out loud. "It's only your imagination."

Dinner was over and she was attempting to do her homework, but no matter how hard she tried, she just couldn't settle down. Maggie was downstairs fooling around in Allison and Sarah's room, and Jenna knew she ought to take advantage of the quiet, but she couldn't focus. She sighed deeply. Then, with renewed determination, she plumped up the pillows on her bed, leaned back into them, balanced her biology book on her bent knees, and tried to concentrate on her reading.

Unfortunately, all she could think about was the weird day she'd had at school. Weird? No, bizarre. She had no idea why, but she was practically certain that people had been looking at her funny all day.

The whole thing had started in homeroom. Nothing too obvious, just a couple of half-embarrassed, half-amused glances—as if her sweater were buttoned up crooked or something. But it *wasn't* buttoned crooked. Jenna had checked. Over and over and over, in fact, as the day wore on and she kept getting those looks.

*Is there something on my face? Is my bra strap showing? Am I getting a zit so huge people can see it across the room?* she'd worried. But the answer to all those questions—and a thousand more just like them—had been no. No, no, no. Jenna had inspected every square inch of her clothing—twice. There was nothing on her face, nothing unusual about her hair, her backpack, her shoes . . . there was no explanation at all.

"You're paranoid," she muttered now, throwing her biology textbook off her lap. "There was nothing wrong with you." There *couldn't* have been. She'd even asked Peter at lunchtime, and he hadn't found a single thing. "Besides, it's not like the whole school was *staring*, or cracking up laughing or anything. It was just a few people you barely even know looking at you funny."

It was going to drive her crazy.

"Do your geometry," she told herself.

Mrs. Wilson had assigned enough homework to take anyone's mind off her problems. Jenna dug through the papers on her bed, looking for the sheet she'd written the assignment on—an old, light blue choir handout. It wasn't there. Jenna hurried nervously over to her desk and shuffled through the mess on top—not there either. She checked her empty backpack, then began digging furiously through all the same papers she'd already ruled out.

After a few minutes, she had to admit defeat. "Great," she groaned. Somehow she'd lost it. She *never* lost things. Now she'd have to get the assignment some other way.

*I could call Miguel,* she thought suddenly, catching her breath. *It would be the perfect excuse.* His phone number was in her steno pad full of Eight Prime notes, along with everyone else's.

*No, don't be an idiot,* she reprimanded herself a moment later. *Miguel's the last person you ought to call. Call Cyn Girard.*

But Jenna didn't want to call her classmate. She didn't want to call *anyone,* in fact, if she couldn't call Miguel.

"Just get it off the computer," she muttered grouchily, grabbing a blank sheet of paper and heading down the stairs toward the den.

Jenna could hear Maggie laughing loudly in Allison and Sarah's room as she sat down to log onto the CCHS Web site. *If I'm lucky, she'll stay in there all night,* she thought. Tuning out the younger girls, Jenna got busy on the computer.

"Please, please, be there," she whispered as the high school's home page appeared on her monitor. Sometimes Mrs. Wilson posted the assignments, and sometimes she didn't. Jenna punched through a series of menu screens until she finally reached her geometry teacher's page.

*Yeah!* she thought when the assignment came up. Jenna copied down the problem numbers, planning to log off and return to her room. As she exited back to the CCHS home page, though, the large guest book icon caught her eye and she couldn't resist clicking on it.

*Just for a minute,* she warned herself, aware from

past experience what a fascinating waste of time the school's guest book could be. Students posted whatever they wanted to there, and it was always full of messages to other students, cryptically or not so cryptically encoded for secrecy. Jenna especially liked the love poems, which were always posted anonymously and usually addressed to the most popular girls at school. Sometimes people would post other poems, too, or short stories they had written. The art and photography students liked to scan their work and upload the digital images. Everything that came in stayed in chronological order, and Jenna paged back through a few screens of items posted earlier that afternoon.

*You need to log off and do your math*, her conscience nagged her, but she ignored it. She wasn't going to stay on long, just a few more screens . . .

Some guy using the code name Lovestud was trying to convince one of the cheerleaders that he was the guy for her. Practically every other message was from him. *Like any self-respecting girl would be interested in the type of loser who calls himself Lovestud!* Jenna thought, but she couldn't help getting drawn in. The guy was persistent, she had to give him that. She was all the way back into yesterday's messages now, and he was still dominating the correspondence.

*You're wasting time*, her conscience nagged again.

"One more minute," Jenna bargained under her breath, "and then I promise I'll log off." She was curious now to see if this weirdo's crush had ever sent him a message back. She paged quickly through the screens . . . scanning . . . scanning . . .

"Oh, *no!*" she screamed, clapping a hand over her mouth. The image filling the screen was so appalling that for a long, frozen moment between beats she actually thought her heart had stopped. All the oxygen fled the room. Jenna gasped for air, her emotions reeling, her eyes still on the monitor. Someone had posted a scanned photograph of *her,* asleep with her mouth open and a pathetically goofy expression on her face.

Jenna closed her eyes, praying she was hallucinating, but when she opened them again, her slack, unconscious face still filled the screen. The pillowcase under her head was the one her grandmother had cross-stitched for her—the one with the fluffy pink sheep—and she was wearing a dumb, little kid's nightgown she should have passed down long ago. Not only that, but her hair was a total mess, and . . .

Oh, please . . . *no!* Was she *drooling?*

With bated breath, she read the caption typed beneath the picture: HI, I'M JENNA CONRAD. I'M A JUNIOR AND I THINK I'M REALLY GREAT!

For a moment Jenna was almost too horrified to speak. No wonder people at school were looking at her funny—she was *ruined!* She hurriedly checked the monitor. The photo had been posted early Tuesday afternoon.

*"Maggie!"* she screeched, finding her voice with a vengeance. The little monster had promised to get her back after their latest argument on Monday. She must have taken a Polaroid that same night, scanned it at school on Tuesday, and posted it when she got home. It had been up for more than twenty-four hours!

"Maggie!" Jenna screamed again.

"What's all this shouting?" Jenna's mother demanded, hurrying into the den. "What's going on?"

Jenna pushed back in the rolling chair, rose unsteadily to her feet, and pointed to the monitor. "Look what Maggie did!"

Mrs. Conrad glanced at the photograph, then bent to examine it more closely. Her auburn eyebrows drew together. "I don't understand. Is that a screen saver or . . . ?"

"No, it's not a screen saver!" Jenna shouted. "She posted that on the *Internet*! The entire *world* has access to that picture." Then anger gave way to humiliation and Jenna started to cry. Tears burst loose in an unexpected torrent, streaming down both cheeks.

"Maggie!" Mrs. Conrad called sternly.

Jenna heard the door of Allison's bedroom creak open, and a moment later Maggie's pale, frightened face peeked through a doorway into the den. Jenna guessed that Allison and Sarah were probably right behind her, listening from the hall.

Maggie swallowed hard, then managed a weak smile. "Yes?"

"Come here," Mrs. Conrad commanded.

Maggie began shuffling across the worn braided rug toward her mother just as Mr. Conrad appeared, bursting into the room from the other side. "What in the world's going on?" he asked. "I could hear Jenna yelling from all the way in the garage."

Mrs. Conrad pointed to the computer screen. "Jenna just found her picture on the Internet." Then, turning to Maggie, Mrs. Conrad made her voice severe. "Did you do this, Maggie?"

Maggie flushed and shifted her weight nervously from foot to foot, her eyes fixed on the rug. "It could have been anyone."

"*Oh!*" Jenna shouted, too outraged to put her thoughts into a sentence.

"Don't you lie to me, Margaret Ellen Conrad," her mother said. "Not *everyone* is running around this house with a camera at night. Now, did you take this picture or didn't you?"

"You'll only make things worse by lying, Maggie," her father added. "If it wasn't you, then it was someone else in this house. And I can assure you I'll find out who."

Jenna glared at her sister, wiping at the tears dropping off her chin. Of course it was Maggie!

She'd never seen anyone more guilty in her life! Maggie's attention was still focused on the floor, but now her spine seemed to melt right in front of them, like the wicked witch when Dorothy doused her with that bucket of water.

"You know you did it, Maggie!" Jenna accused, unable to hold back any longer. "Why don't you just admit it, you chicken little—"

"You deserved it!" Maggie cried, her head jerking up and sparks in her amber eyes. "How *dare* you call my dress ugly—or Scott a dork? You had it coming, Jenna!"

"If you think—" Jenna began irately.

"That's enough!" Mr. Conrad interrupted. "That's *more* than enough, in fact."

The reproach in his tone made it clear how little he thought of both their arguments, and Jenna hung her head, ashamed. She hated disappointing her parents, but lately it seemed as if Maggie kept pushing her into it. If only she didn't have to share a room with the evil little pain . . .

"Margaret, you're grounded," Mrs. Conrad announced. "For one week. No phone calls, no visitors, and you come straight home from school."

Maggie's mouth dropped open. "That's not *fair*! Jenna started it. You don't know what she—"

"That may be," Mr. Conrad cut in sharply. "But we're finishing it. It's one thing to squabble in the house, but you went too far, Maggie. We're a *family*. We don't wash our dirty linen in public."

"We don't mind hanging it out the window!" Maggie cried, but luckily no one but Jenna knew what she meant.

Mr. Conrad gave Maggie a hard look. "You're grounded," he said, echoing his wife. "Starting tomorrow."

"I *can't* start tomorrow!" Maggie protested frantically. "What about the dance? The Fall *Fantasy*! And it was Jenna's fault, anyway—"

"I'm sorry about the dance," Mrs. Conrad cut her off. "I know how much you were looking forward to it. But how can we let you go now, after this? Maybe next time you'll think before you act."

"It wasn't my fault!" Maggie wailed. "Jenna—"

"I said that was *enough*!" Mr. Conrad snapped, his patience finally exhausted. "I'm not going to stand here and listen to you girls tear each other apart. Go to your room, Maggie."

Maggie whirled to face Jenna, tears spilling down her own cheeks now. "Jenna! Jenna, *please* . . ." All her pride and high-and-mighty airs were stripped away as she begged with her eyes for some kind of help. Her little prank had obviously backfired beyond her wildest dreams. For a moment Jenna almost pitied her.

*If I say I forgive her, Mom and Dad might let her go to the dance. . . .* Then Jenna's eyes wandered back

165

to her drooling likeness on the computer screen, and Maggie lost her last chance. *She's got to be kidding!* Jenna thought angrily, shaking her head to Maggie's silent plea. *Who knows how many people saw that photo? Miguel could have seen it!* The mere idea brought on a fresh burst of tears.

Maggie's features collapsed in despair as her final hope deserted her. Her first formal dance, her Fall Fantasy, was lost forever. "I—I *hate* you!" she shouted at Jenna. Then she ran from the room, sobbing violently.

*"Maggie!"* Mrs. Conrad cried, shocked. The only reply was the sound of Maggie's sturdy legs pounding up the stairs and the vicious slam of her bedroom door.

"She didn't mean it," Jenna's mother hurried to assure her, putting a comforting arm around Jenna's shoulders. "We're all just very upset right now, and missing that dance is a big disappointment to Maggie."

Jenna sniffed and wiped her wet face on her shirt.

The way things were going lately, the feeling was pretty mutual.

# Twelve

"So what time am I picking you up tomorrow night?" Nicole asked, trying not to watch as Courtney took a bite from a delicious-looking wedge of homemade chocolate cake. "My mom said I could have the car, and I'd like to get there *on time* this week."

The last football game the two of them had gone to was nearly a disaster because Courtney had been so late. They'd finally found seats, but only in the least desirable part of the bleachers.

"Tomorrow night?" Courtney echoed, swallowing guiltily. "What are we doing tomorrow night?"

"What are we doing tomorrow night?" Nicole repeated sarcastically. "It's only the game against Cave Creek! I'd like to get a seat that isn't in the geek section this time."

Courtney squirmed uncomfortably on their favorite lunchtime bench. "Oh, um, yeah. Did we say we were going to that?"

Nicole stared. "Do I need reservations now? We *always* go to the games together."

"I . . . uh . . . well, I kind of told Jeff I'd go to the game with him."

"You *what*? *Court*ney!"

Courtney put down her cake and wiped her frosting-coated fingers on a wadded paper napkin. "Well, I didn't know you wanted to go—"

"Don't give me that!" Nicole exploded. "I *always* go! We've been to every single home game together since freshman year!"

"Calm down," Courtney said, cringing and glancing around the crowded quad. "Geez."

For once it was Nicole making the scene and Courtney getting embarrassed, but the irony of the situation was lost on Nicole as she ranted on. "You *know* I don't have anyone to go with now. How could you do this to me the day before the game? Now I'm going to miss seeing. . . ." She was so upset, she couldn't even finish the sentence. Besides, they both knew what she meant. *Not* that she cared one way or the other about seeing Jesse play—it was the principle of the thing.

"Okay. I'm sorry, all right?" Courtney said. "Do you think you could calm down now?"

The uncharacteristic apology surprised Nicole into silence. It was a sulky, injured silence all the same.

"Why don't you go with someone else?" Courtney suggested tentatively. "Maybe you can hook up with the God Squad."

Nicole shot her friend a poisonous look.

"Er, I mean Jenna and Peter," Courtney amended, averting her eyes. "They're probably going."

"They probably are," Nicole agreed, "but I can't ask them *now*. I'll look too pathetic."

"Oh, please. They're not going to care."

"*I* care!" Nicole cried.

Suddenly tears brimmed in her eyes. She looked hurriedly down at her lap, trying to blink them back. Her sandwich lay there, blurred out of focus on its paper sack. She'd actually eaten a couple of bites for once.

"You're taking this too hard," Courtney insisted. "It's not that big a deal."

*Easy for you to say*, Nicole thought bitterly. Courtney wasn't the one without a boyfriend, without a date, without even a *girlfriend* to hang out with. Nicole felt like a reject. And even as furious as she was with Jesse, the thought of missing the game was so depressing she could barely stand it.

A second later she was stuffing her half-eaten sandwich back into her lunch bag and angrily wadding the whole thing into a lumpy misshapen ball. *I have to win that modeling contest*, she thought, tossing the result into an overflowing trash can. *It's the only chance I have*.

Jenna climbed slowly up the stairs after school on Thursday, hoping Maggie wasn't in their room, knowing she probably was.

*Of course she's in there—she's grounded.*

Her heart sank a little at the thought of spending another night with her sister like the night before. Maggie had sobbed and sulked and sniffled well into the small hours, refusing to so much as look Jenna's way. This morning—her eyes red and swollen, but her freckled nose firmly back in the air—she'd been queen of the ice princesses. Jenna had never felt so not talked to in her life.

*Who cares?* she thought now, trying to shrug it off. *If I'm lucky, she'll keep it up all week.* Jenna paused with her hand on the bedroom doorknob, listening for sounds from the other side. There was only silence. *No sobbing, anyway.* With a last deep breath, Jenna turned the knob and pushed the door open.

Maggie lay in the fetal position on her twin bed, her face turned toward the wall. She made no move as Jenna walked in. Dropping her backpack onto her own bed, Jenna hesitated a moment, then crossed to the closet to hang up her blazer.

Strangely enough, the double closet doors were already pushed to one side as far as they would go, exposing Jenna's half of the closet. Maggie never closed the sliding doors, but they were always left open on *her* side, not Jenna's. Jenna glanced suspiciously over her shoulder—her sister was still lying perfectly motionless with her back to the room, as if sleeping. Shrugging off her jacket, Jenna reached slowly for a hanger.

There was something weird about the way her clothes were hanging. She couldn't say what, but everything seemed just slightly off. Her shirts and skirts and dresses were all in their proper places . . . were they hanging crooked? Jenna tried to ignore the bad feeling she was getting, but then she glanced down at her shoes. She was positive the brown flats had been in front when she'd left for school that morning. Now they were behind a pair of sneakers.

Jenna's eyes narrowed angrily. "Have you been in my things, Maggie?"

The answer from the bed was an injured sigh.

"Maggie?"

"No! Leave me alone," Maggie said.

"Then why is my side of the closet open? And who moved my shoes?"

"I have no idea."

Her tone was convincing, but Jenna wasn't sure whether to believe her sister or not. She gazed back into her closet, searching for any sure sign of trespassing, but there was nothing definite. She just had this horrid, uneasy feeling . . .

*You're getting paranoid*, she thought. But the next instant she remembered how ready she'd been to write off all those strange stares at school to paranoia, and she became twice as suspicious.

Closing the closet, Jenna walked over to her desk and examined the things on top of it. Her papers all seemed to be there. Her pencil cup, stapler, and battery-powered pencil sharpener were lined up along the back edge, the way she always kept them. But her little china clock was facing straight out into the room instead of slightly toward her chair, as usual. And her dictionary—she liked it on the *right* of her thesaurus, not the left.

"You *have* been going through my things!" she accused.

Maggie said nothing.

"You *have*, you little sneak! What did you take?"

"Nothing!" Maggie screamed, bursting into tears. She leapt onto her feet to face Jenna, her cheeks an angry, mottled red. "Why don't you just leave me alone? Leave me alone and stop picking on me!"

Jenna was shocked to see that her sister's eyes were even more bloodshot than they'd been that morning, and she wondered briefly if Maggie had spent the entire day crying. It didn't seem impossible. *After all, she would have had to tell Scott Jenner she was grounded.* . . .

"Do you swear you didn't take anything, or *do* anything, or . . . or . . . *anything*?" Jenna demanded.

"Go get Mom," Maggie offered at the top of her voice. "I don't care. What else can you do to me, Jenna?"

"I only want to know—"

"Just leave me *alone!*" Maggie howled, throwing herself back onto her bed and sobbing inconsolably.

Jenna watched her sister for several long, suspicious minutes before she sat down on her own small bed. If this was an act, Maggie was going to bring home the Oscar. *Maybe she's telling the truth,* Jenna thought. *Maybe Mom was in here cleaning or something.* On any other day, Jenna wouldn't have given the extremely minor inconsistencies in her room a second look.

*Who knows? Maybe I am getting paranoid.*

Peter stood outside the Conrads' front door after dinner Thursday night, psyching himself up to knock.

*Okay. Nothing to it. All you have to do is ask Jenna if she wants to go out for dinner on Saturday. She'll say yes, because . . . why wouldn't she? So just stay calm or you'll give the whole thing away.*

"The whole thing" involved reservations at an extremely fancy restaurant, after which Peter planned to surprise Jenna with the bracelet. He closed his eyes and tried to imagine kissing her at the end of their very first date, but his heart started pounding so hard that it actually made him feel dizzy. He had to open them up again fast, before he lost his balance. Making a fist with one sweaty hand, he took a deep breath and knocked on the door.

Jenna herself answered almost instantly. "I don't

know what you're doing here, but *boy*, am I glad to see you!" she said in a rush. "Maggie's being such a pain that I can't even stand to be in the same room with her, my parents are watching some deadly boring documentary, and Caitlin's totally hogging the computer—like there's really anything *she* needs to do on it. If I stay in this house another second, I'll go crazy!"

Peter caught the tone, even if he missed half the words. "Ice cream run?" he suggested.

Jenna smiled. "You read my mind. Mom, Dad," she called back over her shoulder, "I'm going for ice cream with Peter." She hurried him off the doorstep and shut the door behind them without waiting for an answer.

"Whew!" she breathed as they walked down the flagstone path to the street. "You must be my knight in metallic blue armor tonight."

"Huh?"

Jenna laughed at his confused expression. "The Toyota," she explained, pointing.

"Oh." They reached the car and Peter opened the passenger door. It was dark on Jenna's street, and the large shade trees seemed to brood and sigh over their impending loss of leaves. Someone else might have found the atmosphere gloomy, but Peter was too nervous and full of plans to notice anything more than the cool fall air.

"So where are we going?" he asked as he let himself into the car and buckled his seat belt.

"You know, I don't even care. Why don't we just drive around for a while and see if someplace incredible occurs to us?"

"Suits me." Peter started the engine. *Ask her now, now, now,* a voice inside him urged as the car rolled down the quiet street. *Do it now before you lose your nerve.*

"It's so good to have a friend like you, Peter," Jenna said suddenly, stretching in her seat. "You don't know what I've been through these last few weeks. I don't think I'd have made it without you."

"You mean what you've been through with Maggie." Jenna had filled him in on every detail of the Internet incident during lunch, and they'd even gone over to the computer lab together to make sure Mrs. Conrad had succeeded in getting the school to remove Maggie's contribution to the guest book. Personally, Peter didn't believe it was possible to take a bad picture of Jenna, but it was gone, in any event—to her obvious relief.

"Yeah. Maggie. And . . ." She shrugged. "You know, everything."

"Everything what? I thought everything else was going pretty well."

"Well . . . you know."

Peter *didn't* know. "Is something the matter?" he asked.

"No!" Jenna said, too quickly. "I mean, you know, there's always *something*. Some little thing. Nothing important."

"Like what?"

"Like . . . well, like I just said—nothing important. I don't want to go into every little thing that bugs me, I only want you to know how much I like having you for a friend."

"Oh." Peter drove silently for the next few miles, turning Jenna's words over and over in his head. Something was obviously bothering her—something *other* than Maggie. Not only that, but hadn't she just said she liked him as a *friend*?

*Perfect*, he thought with a mental groan.

"So what made you come over tonight?" Jenna asked eventually. "I mean, I'm glad you did, but why?"

"Well—I—um," Peter stammered. He wasn't ready to give up his dream date yet, but how could he ask her out now—after what she'd just finished telling him? "I wanted to know if we're going to the Wildcats' game together tomorrow."

Jenna stared as if he were ten cards short of a deck. "Well, *yeah*. We always go to the games together. I . . . just assumed . . ."

"Good. Yeah. Right," Peter said quickly. "Just checking." His heart was pounding again, and his sweaty palms made sticky, squelching noises on the plastic steering wheel. Why did none of his little conversations with Jenna ever go the way he planned?

*I'll ask her out tomorrow, during the football game,* he decided. *There'll be plenty of time then. Besides, it won't seem as suspicious if I do it in a crowd.*

He sighed, hoping he was right. Becoming Jenna's boyfriend was turning out to be almost more stress than he could take.

# Thirteen

"How's this?" Miguel asked, stopping beside a half-full bench near the top of the bleachers.

Leah shrugged. "Fine. Anywhere is fine with me." Even though it was the very first football game Leah had ever attended, she wasn't particularly concerned about getting a good view of the field. She wasn't even sure how much she'd be *watching* the field, with Miguel sitting right beside her.

The two of them edged down the row to take seats next to a group of adults in green CCHS Boosters jackets, and Miguel immediately scooted around on the bench to face her. "Is this good?" he asked anxiously.

"Perfect." Leah leaned into his shoulder and tickled him playfully in the ribs. "Almost as perfect as you are."

"Leah!" Miguel whispered, a blush creeping into his cheeks. "Not here."

"Not here what?" she teased.

"You promised," he reminded her.

Leah chuckled and sat back in her seat. "Oh, all

right. I was just testing your resolve." She didn't want to make out in front of the entire student body either. It was enough that they were there together—even if they *were* sitting way at the top of the bleachers, determined to spend the game acting like casual friends.

"Anyway, I thought you wanted to see the game," said Miguel. "You'd better behave or I'll get you for it later."

"I can hardly wait," Leah replied with a mischievous wink.

Miguel shook his head and turned his attention to the field, apparently determined to ignore her innuendoes. Leah sighed and braced herself for two or more hours of near-total boredom.

Down on the grass, the players were running around like demented ants. She and Miguel had apparently missed something called the kickoff, and the game was already under way. Leah knew Jesse was out there somewhere, but the guys all looked the same in their green jerseys and gold helmets; she couldn't make him out. Melanie was easier to spot, her blond hair shining as she called cheers with the rest of the squad. It was the first time Leah had ever seen the cheerleaders in battle, and she watched for a while, far more interested in them than the game.

"There's Melanie," she said, pointing for Miguel. "I can't find Jesse."

"He's number eighty-nine," Miguel told her, pointing in a different direction. "Right there."

"If you say so." Leah wasn't a bit convinced it was possible to recognize a person under all that heavy gear. She gazed down at the player Miguel alleged was Jesse, her mind already wandering.

*I wish we'd had an Eight Prime meeting last night. That's always fun.* It hadn't escaped her that there'd been a little too much arguing at the last one, but then again, that was to be expected in a group of such different personalities. *If it hadn't been for Kurt Englbehrt's carnival, there's no way we'd have met at all,* she thought, not for the first time.

She wondered whether Kurt's girlfriend, Dana, was in the bleachers somewhere. It didn't seem likely. Leah had barely seen the pretty blonde since Kurt's memorial service, and the rumor going around school was she was taking his death really hard.

*At least we have Eight Prime to help us feel like Kurt lives on. Maybe donating a bus isn't much, but it shows Kurt's life was important. I can't wait to see the pumpkins that Peter and Jenna—*

"Oh, no!" she gasped. "Oh, I can't believe it."

"What?" asked Miguel.

"I forgot to talk to Principal Kelly today. I mean, I didn't *forget*—I went by his office. But he was busy and the secretary told me to come back later . . . and *then* I forgot."

Miguel shrugged, his eyes relieved. "I think we'll all survive. We don't even have the pumpkins yet."

"But I *never* forget to do things. Everyone's going to think I'm an airhead."

"I doubt it," Miguel said, smiling.

"I'll call him this weekend," Leah said. "Tomorrow."

"At *home*? I'm not sure that's such a good idea."

"Why not? I told you he's a friend of my parents—he won't be mad."

"Maybe not. But it's not like you need to know right this second, either. Ask him on Monday. You know he'll say yes."

Leah nodded reluctantly. Miguel's argument made sense. There was no point bothering Principal Kelly just because she had a guilty conscience. Besides, Leah could think of better things to do with her weekend than talk to the school principal.

"You want to go jogging tomorrow?" she asked.

"What?" Miguel cast a bewildered sideways glance her way, then shook his head in disbelief. His eyes returned to the field. "Sure. Whatever."

"Should I pick you up? Say eight o'clock?"

"Huh? Oh. No! Uh, that's not going to work." She suddenly had his full attention. "I just remembered I've got something to do tomorrow."

"What?"

"What? Um . . . well . . . water polo practice."

"On Saturday morning?" Leah asked skeptically.

181

"Well, it's not an *official* practice. It's just a few of the guys getting together at the pool to go over some drills. I'd skip it, but I already promised to be there. It's too late to cancel now."

"Hmm," Leah said, narrowing her eyes. *That's quite possibly the lamest excuse I've ever heard*, she thought.

And then she realized something. Miguel was *never* available early on Saturday mornings. At the carnival he'd been the only guy who didn't volunteer to show up early to help with the booth. At the car wash, he'd not only insisted on starting late with the signs, he'd shown up even later. And just now jogging had been fine with him—until Leah mentioned picking him up at eight. What was going on? Leah liked thinking she and Miguel were keeping secrets from everyone else, but now she was starting to wonder. Was Miguel keeping secrets from her, too?

"Let's go jogging *Sunday* morning," Miguel suggested, breaking into her thoughts. "I don't have anything planned all day."

Did his voice sound the slightest bit guilty? Leah wasn't sure.

"All right, then," she agreed slowly. "But how about brunch instead? My parents invited you to come with us."

"They did? Well . . . I . . . uh . . ."

Leah stared him down, daring him to back out of two invitations in a row.

"That sounds great," he finished weakly.

"Good. We'll pick you up at ten. Don't forget to give me your address tonight."

"You don't need to pick me up," Miguel protested. "I wouldn't want to take your parents so far out of their way."

"I thought you said you lived downtown."

"Well, yeah. But I'll just drive over to your house. It'll be easier."

Leah was about to debate that point when the booster club on Miguel's other side leapt to its feet, screaming with excitement. Everyone in the stands was roaring, in fact. The noise level was amazing.

"Oh, no! A touchdown!" Miguel groaned, squeezing his head between both hands. "A touchdown and we *missed* it!" He closed his eyes, a pained expression on his face.

*Okay, I'll let him drive over to meet us*, Leah decided quickly, afraid if she argued any more he'd blame missing the goal on her.

*I'll let him drive this time.*

"Did you see that touchdown? That was *great!*" Peter yelled, cheering with the crowd.

Jenna clapped and whistled loudly at his side, but her heart wasn't in the game. Sure, the Wildcats were ahead, but their performance so far that night hadn't been anywhere near as exciting as during their season opener. Not exciting enough to make Jenna forget her problems with Maggie, for instance, and not *nearly* exciting enough to get her mind off the fact that Leah and Miguel were sitting together at the top of the bleachers. They were playing it cool, trying to act like casual acquaintances, but Jenna knew better. She couldn't even bring herself to point them out to Peter.

The Wildcats blasted in the kick for the extra point and the crowd cheered again. Then Cave Creek took possession and people started dropping back into their seats, Jenna among the first. She wanted to enjoy herself—she was *trying* to enjoy herself—but she just wasn't having any fun. It was taking all her effort simply to keep Peter from guessing how unhappy she was.

*At least being here is better than staying home with Maggie the Martyr*, she thought, forcing herself not to look up the bleachers again. By the time Peter had arrived to drive Jenna to the game, Maggie was crying so hard about missing the Fall Fantasy that she'd actually thrown up her dinner. She'd kept checking the clock, saying things like "Now I'd be getting ready," "Now Scott would be leaving his house," "Now he'd be pinning on my corsage." Then she'd burst into tears and have to run for the bathroom again. Needless to say, it wasn't a pretty sight. It had taken plenty of self-control on Jenna's part to keep from feeling sorry for the little whiner.

Jenna's attention was temporarily distracted by the unlikely sight of Nicole's friend Courtney strolling along the wide walkway at the base of the bleachers, arm in arm with Jeff Nguyen. *Courtney and Jeff?* Jenna thought, shaking her head in astonishment. *And where's Nicole?*

"Isn't that . . . ?" Peter began hesitantly at her side. Jenna could tell by the shock in his voice that he too had spotted the odd couple.

"I'm as amazed as you are."

"But Jeff's so *quiet*."

"He used to be."

Peter and Jenna had been friendly with Jeff in junior high, but in the last couple of years they'd drifted apart. They still talked in the halls from time to time, though, and loud, wild Courtney Bell was the last person Jenna would have expected him to be attracted to. *Just wait until he brings* her *home*, she couldn't help thinking, imagining how Jeff's conservative Vietnamese parents would react to the sight of the provocatively dressed redhead clinging to their oldest son.

"Opposites attract, I guess," she muttered at last, returning her gaze to the game.

"Yeah." Peter shook his head.

"Hey, Jenna," he added suddenly. "Do you want to do something tomorrow night? I was thinking we could . . . uh . . . well . . . how about miniature golf?"

Jenna bit the inside of her lip but still managed a cheerful smile. "Sure. Why not?" She didn't want Peter to know she could barely keep from crying.

What was *wrong* with her? Why didn't anyone ever ask *her* on a date? Leah was out with the man of Jenna's dreams, and now Courtney had a great guy too. All around her, in fact, the stands were jammed with happy, excited couples. Meanwhile, the most exciting thing *Jenna* could manage was miniature golf with her best friend.

Miniature golf!

*Leave it to Peter,* she thought, with one last miserable glance at Miguel. *Mr. Romance.*


"Are you nervous?" Tanya asked Melanie as the cheerleaders lined up for the halftime show.

Melanie's reply was a sickly grin. Nervous? She felt as if she might pass out. The stands were packed, and the squad's new stunt was only a few minutes away. Melanie's entire world seemed to be compressing into a swath of green grass and a miniature black trampoline.

"Ready?" Vanessa shouted suddenly.

"Okay!" the squad fired back. They began marching to the center of the field, the fists on their hips gripping green-and-gold pom-poms. It was now or never. Melanie could barely breathe.

As if in a dream, she reached the fifty-yard line with the rest of the squad and launched into the short opening cheer. Then the P.A. system began booming out music and the cheerleaders started to dance—a long, rocking number that had the huge crowd stomping in the stands. The stunt with the spirit pyramid was supposed to be the big finale; Melanie could feel the fake smile freezing on her face as every beat of the music brought that moment closer. *This is either going to be the biggest triumph or the most public failure of my entire school career,* she realized, and for a moment it occurred to her to wonder if that wasn't what Vanessa had had in mind all along.

The music ended. A drumroll from the marching band in the end zone had the effect of sudden machine-gun fire on Melanie's shattered nerves. She was desperate to call the whole thing off, to call some other cheer, but the other girls were forming up the pyramid. It was too late to back out now. They were already in position . . . waiting . . .

She backed up in line with the trampoline, her eyes darting frantically around her. The audience was waiting too . . .

With a sharp intake of breath, Melanie began to run. *Don't think about it. Don't think about it. Go, go, go!*

And then she was flying up through the air, her arc high and on target. Her knees tucked into her chest, the flip took control of her body, and she heard the crowd roar with excitement. Her legs kicked out at exactly the proper instant and her feet began straining down for the backs below them. There was an agonizing half-second drop, and then Melanie landed squarely—*perfectly*—on top of the spirit pyramid. Her arms flew skyward in an emphatic V as the stands burst into tumultuous applause.

"*Yes!*" Melanie shouted, knowing she'd made the entire thing look easier than breathing. "Go, Wildcats!"

People were actually up on their feet to cheer her—something they usually did only for the players. The thrill—the rush—was enormous. Melanie grinned triumphantly down at Tanya, who flashed her a smiling thumbs-up. The next thing she knew, Melanie was leaping off the pyramid and the cheerleaders' contribution to halftime was over. She marched off the field with springs in her legs, her adrenaline still pumping.

*That was great! You were brilliant!* she congratulated herself. *What were you so worried about?*

People shouted her name as the cheerleaders passed in front of the stands. Melanie waved to them happily, in total disregard of the dirty looks she was getting from Vanessa. They passed Ms. Carson, who hurried to the rail to congratulate them all and whisper a few words to Vanessa. Finally they reached their seats on the bench. The other cheerleaders immediately wriggled around to face Melanie.

"That was awesome!" Lou Anne exclaimed. "You should have seen it from the ground."

"No kidding," Tanya agreed. "You looked like a total pro."

"That'll show Red River who's boss!" Sue bragged, high-fiving Cindy.

"My dad's going to have the whole thing on tape," Angela said excitedly. "I can barely wait to watch it."

Even Tiffany had to admit that Melanie's landing had been "lighter than usual." Melanie beamed through praise and half-praise alike as the marching band went through its paces.

Then the halftime show was over and the players took the field again. Melanie saw Jesse run by as the cheerleaders rushed to form up at the fifty-yard line.

*I wish he'd seen me do that flip*, she thought, a wry smile on her lips. Unlike his stellar performance during the season opener, Jesse had had some problems in the first half of this game, and Melanie imagined that the sight of her big triumph would have doubly annoyed him as a result. After all, at the last game the crowd had cheered for *Jesse*.

*No danger of that tonight*, Melanie added, her smile growing. Jesse hadn't done anything to actually cost the Wildcats points yet, but he *had* made some embarrassing mistakes. Melanie knew he was probably still stinging about that first-quarter incompletion, for instance. *It couldn't have happened to a nicer guy*, she gloated silently, reveling in the thought of so *much* damaged pride.

"We've Got Spirit!" Vanessa cried loudly, calling the name of the next cheer.

Melanie launched into the cheer enthusiastically, forgetting all about Jesse in her impassioned attempts to encourage CCHS to shout down the visiting fans in the "away" bleachers.

The rest of the game went by slowly. The Wildcats seemed even flatter in the second half than they had in the first, barely managing to hold their slim lead. At the end of the fourth quarter, they finally seemed to remember why they'd come, scoring two flashy touchdowns almost back to back. When the show was over, the fans filed out of the stands satisfied, and Melanie went to the gym to shower and change.

"Are you going to the victory party?" Angela asked as Melanie put the finishing touches on her makeup. She and Angela were the last two cheerleaders in the gym.

Melanie shrugged. She'd intended to when she'd started getting dressed, but now that the rush of her halftime success had passed, she wasn't in the mood. "I don't know. How about you?"

"I promised my mother I'd be home early

tonight," Angela said. "If you want, I'll give you a ride."

"Really? That would be great." She probably could have gotten a ride home from someone at the party just as easily, but Melanie didn't much like parties anymore. And for some reason she found the noise, smoke, and phoniness of the Wildcats' after-game celebrations particularly depressing. Aside from the chance to take a few well-timed shots at Jesse, she couldn't imagine she'd enjoy this one any more than she had the others. She shut her locker and padlocked the door. "I'm ready if you are," she said.

She and Angela had barely left the gym, however, when a tall male figure crashed out of the bushes at the side of the path, lurching toward them in the darkness. Angela screamed, and Melanie was on the verge of bolting in panic when she recognized their attacker's self-satisfied chuckle.

"Jesse!" she cried angrily. "What do you think you're doing?"

"I thought you might want to go to the victory party with me." He stood in the middle of the sidewalk, his legs braced apart to more completely block their way and his green letterman's jacket falling back off his shoulders.

"Think again!" Melanie said furiously. "You scared us half to death." She tried to push past him, but Jesse caught her by the wrists and pulled her toward him.

"Now, that's more like it." He wasn't hurting her, but he wasn't letting go, either, and his grip was too strong to break. Up close, Melanie could smell the dew-damp wool of his jacket and the soap he'd used after the game.

Angela backed away. "Do you two, uh, want to be alone?" she asked uncertainly.

"No!" Melanie said sharply.

"She means yes. See you, Angela." Jesse let go of one of Melanie's wrists to wave Angela toward the parking lot.

"No, stay, Angela!" Melanie cried, wrenching her other wrist free. She backed up quickly, stepping out of Jesse's reach. "I already told you I'm not going anywhere with you, Jesse."

Jesse shrugged, then dropped his voice and leaned forward, looking directly into her eyes. "I figured it out."

"Figured *what* out?"

"I know why you're mad at me now. It's because of what happened between me and Nicole. You're mad because I kissed Nicole, aren't you?"

"Bravo!" Melanie returned sarcastically, clapping with the tips of three fingers in the palm of her other hand. She had intended the gesture to insult him, but Jesse beamed triumphantly.

"I *knew* it! You're jealous!"

"I'm . . . *Oh!* . . . You're . . . ," Melanie sputtered, not even sure where to start. That was as much as she had time for, though, because the next second Jesse lunged forward and grabbed her again, pulling her into a passionate embrace.

"Okay, well, I guess I'm leaving now," Angela murmured, apparently assuming she was caught in a lovers' quarrel. "I'll, uh, see you two later."

Melanie heard her friend's footsteps hurrying down the walkway. Quickly, before Jesse could tighten his grip, she brought her fists up under her chin, using her elbows to maintain a half inch of space between their bodies.

"Let go of me," she said, her voice as dangerous as she could make it. "Let go of me, or I swear I'll—"

"You'll what?" Jesse laughed. "Kiss me?"

He stooped to bring his face to hers. Melanie strained backward, turning her head to the side.

"Aw, come on," Jesse whispered, his lips nibbling her ear. "You know you want to."

"You're seriously deluded." His mouth was only inches from hers, his lips still straining to kiss her. And now, for the first time, a familiar smell reached Melanie's nose.

"You—You're drunk!" she accused furiously. Of course! She, of all people, should have recognized the signs. With a burst of angry strength she pushed herself out of Jesse's arms, then faced him down scornfully, her hands on her hips.

"I am not," he lied.

"Do you think I'm an idiot? That I don't recognize the smell of liquor on someone's breath?"

"Geez, calm down."

"Calm down yourself!" Melanie dodged around him and started running for the parking lot, but she'd taken only a few steps when Jesse grabbed her hand from behind, spinning her around.

"All right!" he conceded. "I might have had a couple of shots. To celebrate our win. You know, my dad was in the stands tonight . . ."

"You were drinking with your *father?*"

Jesse grimaced. "Of course not. Just one or two shots by myself. It's not a federal case."

"No, it's just stupid."

Jesse snorted. "Like *you're* so perfect. I may be the new kid in town, but I've heard a few things about you—things I'll bet you don't think I know."

Melanie stiffened apprehensively. "Like what?"

"I think you *know* what," Jesse said, smiling maliciously. With a sharp, unexpected jerk on the hand he still held, he pulled her to him again, pressing his body against hers. "Kiss me and I won't spread it around."

Melanie felt the heat of his breath on her cheeks. The smell of alcohol was overpowering as his mouth neared hers. She closed her eyes for the briefest of moments, trying to clear her confusion. Jesse was lying. He had to be. With all the strength in her tiny frame, Melanie drew back her free right hand and slapped him hard across his drunken face.

"Hey!" he howled, dropping his grip in surprise. He raised a protective hand to his injured cheek, but not before Melanie saw the bright red imprint of her fingers on his skin.

She stared a moment, stunned by the unexpected violence of her action. Then she turned her back and raced down the path, calling out for Angela.

# *Fourteen*

Peter stood nervously on the hardwood floor inside the Conrads' front door, waiting for Sarah to fetch Jenna. The restaurant reservations were confirmed, the bracelet was in his pocket, and the old Toyota outside had been washed and polished to a surprising shine. The only thing that wasn't completely ready was him. His stomach was so jumpy with anxiety that it felt like he'd swallowed a kitten, and his palms were slick with sweat. He was in the process of wiping them on his slacks when Jenna appeared at the top of the stairs. Peter immediately sucked in his breath and stood up straighter, determined to start the evening right.

"You're awfully dressed up for miniature golf!" she commented, looking him over strangely as she reached the bottom of the stairs. Jenna was wearing old jeans and a flannel shirt with a thick denim blue sweater that matched her eyes.

Peter glanced down at his own sharply pressed trousers and polished shoes and wished he'd told her the truth instead of that lame golf story. Personally, he didn't care how Jenna dressed, but he hoped they'd let her into the restaurant that way. "Well, I, uh, told you we'd get something to eat first," he reminded her. "You didn't eat dinner yet, did you?"

"No. But I figured we'd be getting corn dogs at the golf course or something. Are we going to a restaurant?"

"Would you like to?"

Jenna shrugged. "As long as I don't have to change."

Peter smiled weakly.

"I mean, you do have other clothes in the car, right? You're not going to play miniature golf in those shoes."

*Tell her the truth*, a voice in Peter's head urged. *Tell her you're taking her to Le Papillon. She's going to kill you if you let her go dressed like that.*

"Jenna . . . ," he began, but at that instant Maggie came flying down the stairs, her curls a wild river behind her.

"Did you take my Clue CD?" she demanded breathlessly of Jenna, not even glancing at Peter.

"Please!" Jenna said scornfully. "What would I want with that piece of trash?"

"That's what *I'd* like to know! You have it, Jenna. I know you do!" Maggie accused furiously.

Peter watched the exchange in stunned amazement. He knew those two weren't getting along, but he'd never seen them argue so nastily before.

Maggie's eyes flashed an angry warning, and the look in *Jenna's* . . . If he hadn't known better, Peter would almost have said they hated each other.

"Why don't you try looking through that garbage dump on your side of the room?" Jenna suggested snidely. "It's probably under last month's dirty underwear."

"My side isn't messy!"

"Compared to what?" Jenna countered. "A bomb site? Why don't you look in that pit of a closet?"

"My closet—"

"You're a pig and you know it, Maggie! I don't have your stupid CD, so find it yourself."

Maggie's cheeks flamed with anger and humiliation as she faced Jenna from the bottom stair. She glanced briefly at Peter, then tossed her head defiantly. "Well, I know where I *don't* have to look!" she announced loudly, turning back to her sister. "I don't have to look in your desk!"

Jenna's face went as white as her sister's was red. "You'd better stay out of my desk," she warned in a low, tense voice.

"And I *particularly* don't have to look in your bottom desk drawer," Maggie continued, "because I *know* there's no room in there. Not with your stupid love letter about Miguel del Rios taking up all that space!"

"Maggie!" Jenna screamed. Maggie turned and fled up the stairs.

Peter felt as if someone had hit him in the gut with a two-by-four. Jenna and Miguel del Rios?

*It's just another of Maggie's stupid tricks,* he told himself. *Boy, is Jenna ever going to be hot now!* His eyes invited, then begged her to deny it as she slowly turned to face him. But instead of yelling the expected outraged denials, Jenna took one slow, stunned look at his face and exploded into tears, running off in a fit of sobs. A door slammed somewhere upstairs, and Peter was alone.

He stood there a moment, the shock overwhelming. *Jenna and Miguel?* It couldn't be. He'd never seen them anywhere together . . . couldn't remember Jenna ever even talking about Miguel. Maggie's accusation was ridiculous.

And yet there was no denying Jenna's reaction just now.

*Well, I guess you got your wish, Altmann,* Peter thought bitterly as reality sank in. *Jenna's in love, all right. Just not with you.*

His right hand went to his jacket pocket and clutched the pink gift-wrapped box he'd put there so excitedly only an hour before. He felt the tiny bow crush beneath the pressure of his grip, but what difference did it make now? He'd never get to give it to her.

And then the worst thought of all broke over him like a cold, suffocating wave: *Jenna wanted Miguel to give her this bracelet. She must have been thinking about Miguel in the store that day. And the worst part is, you thought you were so smart to get it for her!*

What an idiot he was! He spun around and fumbled with the doorknob. The door flew open and he stumbled blindly into the chill night air, tears burning his eyelids.

Peter felt like flinging the bracelet as far out into the blackness as he could, or—better yet—laying a tire track of squealing rubber over it, crushing that little golden heart as thoroughly as Jenna had just broken his.

He felt like he might throw up.

He felt like nothing between him and Jenna would ever be the same.


Jenna lagged behind the other members of the choir in putting away her heavy white robe. Last night had been the longest night of her life. She'd barely slept for crying, and as she'd tossed and turned, there'd been plenty of time to realize how much of what had happened to her had been her own dumb fault.

Tears threatened to spill over again even now when she remembered that embarrassing scene in front of Peter—her sister shouting out the secret Jenna had guarded so carefully for two entire years. But Jenna no longer blamed Maggie for her troubles. She wasn't *happy* with Maggie, but what could she really expect? Looking back on the all-out war she'd started over a stupid bra, all Jenna could do was wish she were standing in her room again with that offensive pink garment still in her hands. This time she really *would* turn the other cheek. This time she really *would* put it in the hamper—or at least throw it back over to Maggie's side.

A tear dripped off her chin and Jenna wiped her face with both hands, sniffling in the strangely comforting presence of the familiar choir robes. It didn't matter how much losing her chance with Miguel had hurt; where her family was concerned, she'd been selfish, and stupid, and just plain wrong. She saw that now. Not only that, but she didn't know how she was going to face Peter. Here, at least, in the sanctuary of this back room, she knew there was someone with her who understood everything in her heart. Who knew every petty thought she'd ever had, and loved her anyway.

*Dear God*, she prayed silently. *I'm so sorry for the way I acted. Next time, please help me remember to treat Maggie the way I would want to be treated. Well, actually, I did kind of remember. Please help me to do it next time. In Jesus' name, amen.*

Jenna opened her eyes and dried her wet face on the sleeve of her dress, feeling slightly better. At least she hadn't ratted on Maggie for going through her desk. She could have gotten her sister in a lot of trouble for that, but she'd finally come to her senses.

*I started it, and I have to end it. No more fighting with Maggie*, she vowed. After all, hadn't she already made Maggie miss the Fall Fantasy—practically the biggest event in junior high? Jenna had tried so hard to convince herself that her sister had *deserved* to miss the dance, but now she felt horribly guilty. *I could have said something. I could have told Mom and Dad what I did to Maggie's underwear. . . .*

"Jenna, are you coming?" her mother called from the doorway.

Jenna whirled around, startled. "Coming, Mom."

Mrs. Conrad took a long, concerned look at her daughter as Jenna hurried toward her. "Are you all right, dear?"

"Fine." Jenna felt tears welling up again and fought to hold them back.

"You're not still fighting with Maggie, are you?"

"No. No, that's all over."

"I'm glad to hear it." Mrs. Conrad smiled tenderly and smoothed a stray strand of Jenna's hair. "Come on, then. Everyone's waiting for us."

Jenna followed her mother through the back of the church and out into a cool gray morning. As she had feared, Peter was waiting in their usual place at the edge of the front pavement, next to the wrought-iron bench.

*Better get it over with*, she thought. Squaring her

shoulders, she took a deep, calming breath and walked through the courtyard to join him. "Hi."

"Hi," he returned, not meeting her eyes. For some reason, he seemed as embarrassed as she was.

"Listen, Peter," she said in a rush, her voice low and her back to the milling crowd outside the church. "I'm really embarrassed about last night. And I'm sorry about dinner and miniature golf and . . . everything. Do you think we can forget it ever happened?"

"Forget what?" He pushed a hand through his thick blond hair. "You mean you and Mi—?"

"Exactly," she interrupted hurriedly. "Of all the stupid things I've ever done, getting a crush on Miguel del Rios has got to top the list."

"A *crush*?" Peter echoed.

"Well . . . yeah. I thought that was what we were talking about."

Peter looked confused. *Wasn't he paying attention last night?* Jenna wondered.

"But I never told *anyone*," she added in a rush. "*Miguel* doesn't even know, and I'll die if he finds out. You're not going to say anything, are you?" She searched her friend's face hopefully, pleading with her eyes.

"Miguel doesn't *know*?" Peter repeated, still three beats behind the music. "How do you expect to get together with the guy if he doesn't even know you like him?"

Jenna grimaced. "How do you just come out and tell someone something like that? I was trying to work my way around to it. And then, before I even got a chance, I found out he's seeing Leah."

"Leah?" Peter sat down heavily on the bench behind him, the expression on his face completely unreadable.

"I'm afraid so," Jenna said unhappily, taking a seat beside him. "But don't tell anyone about that either, okay? I think they're trying to keep it a secret."

"I don't think they're even together!"

"I *know* they are." Jenna could still call up the memory of the two of them kissing whenever she closed her eyes, but she didn't feel like discussing her evidence. "Take my word for it."

Peter shook his head. "Why didn't you *tell* me you liked Miguel? Didn't you think I could keep a secret?"

"I just . . . it didn't . . . I couldn't."

"But, how *long*?" Peter demanded. "How long have you felt this way?"

"I don't know. A while." The weird way Peter was acting, it seemed better to leave things vague. Jenna's eyes roamed the thinning crowd of parishioners—her parents would be calling her to go home any second. "Do you think we can drop it now?"

But Peter's eyes held her stubbornly. "Do you love him?"

"Oh, Peter . . . I don't know."

"Well, do you still feel the same way? Even though he's dating Leah?"

"You can't tell anyone that they're—"

"I'm not going to tell anyone!" he interrupted impatiently. "I'm not going to tell anyone *anything*, all right? Just answer the question."

Jenna didn't *want* to answer the question, but Peter was staring her down. "I don't know," she said with a sigh. "I guess you don't forget something like that overnight. Not after two whole years of—"

"Two *years*!" Peter yelped.

*Oh, perfect,* Jenna thought, mentally kicking herself for her careless slip of the tongue. Still, maybe it was better this way, with no more secrets between them. "Now you know," she said, sick to death of the entire subject. "Now you know *everything*."

The suspicious look on Peter's face was like nothing she'd ever seen.

"If you say so," he replied.

# Fifteen

Melanie rushed out of the girls' room at lunchtime on Monday, knowing she was already supposed to be in the quad. She was hurrying down the main hall to join the other cheerleaders when Jesse hustled into her path from the door of an open classroom.

"Hi, Melanie," he said, as if nothing at all were the matter between them.

She hadn't seen him since Friday, when she'd slapped him, and as richly as he'd deserved that, she'd thought he'd be a little more upset. She stared a moment, surprised by his apparent amnesia, then tossed her head.

"Get out of my way, Jesse," she said coldly. "I'm *really* not speaking to you now." She sidestepped around him, half expecting him to grab her again, but he let her go by, following on her heels like a lonely stray dog.

"Listen, Melanie, I know you're mad about Friday night. You deserve to be. I . . . I'm sorry. I don't know what—"

"Save your breath, Jesse. And get just one thing straight for once. I'm not interested, I'll never *be* interested, and I want you to leave me alone. All right? Is that pretty clear?"

"Melanie . . ."

"No!" she said angrily. "I've had enough of you." She walked faster to get away from him, then pushed out the door of the main building and into the lunchtime crowd in the quad.

She was still so furious with Jesse that whenever she thought about Friday night she felt like slapping him all over again. *It figures he would wait until now to try his pathetic apology*, she thought. *Right before the spirit rally.*

Melanie struggled to force Jesse from her mind and a smile to her lips as she hurried to join the rest of her squad. The minitrampoline was already in place near the center of the quad, and the cheerleaders stood scanning the crowd with worried expressions, no doubt looking for her.

"Here I am!" Melanie called, beginning to run.

"Finally!" she heard Tiffany say huffily to Vanessa.

Vanessa's small eyes glared as Melanie reached the other girls. "You're late," she said accusingly. "We've all been waiting for you."

"Sorry. I had to stop off in the girls' room, and then I . . . uh . . . got held up."

"I *told* you I wanted to do this right at noon, so we'd have time to eat lunch afterward."

"I know. I'm sorry," Melanie said, careful not to show how weary she was of her captain's bossiness.

Vanessa gave her one last nasty look, then turned to the rest of the squad. "All right. Is *everyone* ready now?"

The other girls nodded solemnly, and Melanie had to work to keep from rolling her eyes. They were only doing one short dance and the new flip onto the spirit pyramid. Vanessa had dreamed up the idea the night before to keep people fired up about the Wildcats' two-and-zero season. It was going to take five minutes, tops, but the way Vanessa was carrying on, a person would think they were opening on Broadway.

"All right, Lou Anne," Vanessa directed. "Turn on the music."

Lou Anne hefted an enormous boom box onto the raised metal roof of a nearby trash can, and, at a nod from Vanessa, pushed the Play button. Music blared out, filling the quad. People started moving back to give the girls some room, forming a ring in the center of the quad that rapidly filled in from behind.

Melanie spotted Jenna and Peter near the front of the crowd. Then, out of the corner of her eye, she noticed that Jesse had pushed to the front as well, along with a few other Wildcats. Their eyes met as Melanie took her place on the end of the line and, for a fraction of a second, she saw something in Jesse's face that threw her into confusion. Then the introductory music ended, the main song started, and the cheerleaders began to dance.

Melanie's smile was big and lighthearted as she kept step with the other girls. The deception cost her no effort—she was an expert at faking smiles. No one watching from the crowd could have guessed how conflicted she suddenly felt. She took advantage of a turn with the music to glance Jesse's way again.

Was she going crazy? If she didn't know better, Melanie would have sworn that someone had just hit the guy where he lived. His straight brown brows gathered low over dejected blue eyes, and his lips pursed strangely over a chin tucked into his chest. There wasn't a trace of his usual cockiness as he pouted at the front of the circle. On the contrary, the guy looked absolutely crushed.

*Did I do that?* Melanie wondered, awed. It was amazing to think she might have actually gotten through to him. Then Jesse looked right at her and she knew for sure that she had. His square jaw jutted out defiantly and he pulled himself up to full height before he spun around and pushed his way back through the crowd, away from the quad. Away from her. . . .

*So what?* Melanie thought. *Good!*

She tried to forget about Jesse as the cheerleaders

finished their dance. The music reached its climax, then came to a sudden, dramatic end. The cheerleaders hit their last pose and broke into spontaneous displays of spirit, leaping and flipping.

"Go, Wildcats!" Melanie shouted, ending with a flurry of straddle jumps.

The crowd applauded wildly. Vanessa let them carry on awhile; then she held up her hand for a chance to speak.

"If you were at the game last week," she shouted, "you already saw our latest twist on the spirit pyramid. But for those of you who missed it, we're going to give you another chance right now!"

The applause became even more enthusiastic as the cheerleaders began to form the pyramid. Melanie backed up and waited for the other girls to get into position, a distracted half smile on her face.

*I can't believe Jesse was so upset,* she thought. *He probably wasn't even thinking about me.* But then she remembered the proud, embarrassed way Jesse had reacted when he'd caught her looking at him, and she knew better. He *had* to have been thinking about her.

The rest of the squad was ready. Melanie gauged the distance between herself and the trampoline, and the trampoline and the top of the pyramid. She took a few extra steps backward, her mind not really on the stunt as she lined up for her run. *Maybe I was too hard on him. . . .*

*Forget about Jesse!* she thought angrily the next second. Why was she worried about him after the way he'd treated her? She *hoped* she'd hurt his feelings. An instant later she was running over the pavement, her eyes fixed straight ahead.

Melanie hit the trampoline with all her strength, fury putting an added spring into her bounce. The crowd roared as she shot into the air, but Melanie barely heard it. The rotation on her flip was tight, fast, mechanical. *I wonder where he went?*

The unexpected early impact of her feet with Tiffany's and Cindy's lower backs sent a shudder up Melanie's legs. She had opened out of her flip too soon—her weight was too far back. She windmilled frantically with her arms, but the stunt was unrecoverable. She felt the pyramid shudder off balance as her footing failed her and her shoes skidded forward along the backs of the top two girls. Melanie buckled at the waist. Her head snapped down toward her feet even as her hips slipped off the back side of the pyramid. Then her head came up and she was falling backward, only empty air between her and the concrete below.

"*Melanie!*" Tanya screamed, running toward her.

But Tanya was on the wrong side of the pyramid. She dropped out of sight almost as soon as Melanie became aware of her. Melanie grasped frantically for something to break her fall, but there was nothing there, nothing to hold on to. For a second—one

211

surreal, slow-motion second—she saw the horrified, gaping faces of the students in the quad, felt her body rotating backward out of control, and knew there was no way to stop what was about to happen.

"Melanie!"

The back of her head hit the pavement with an impact that exploded in a shock wave of red behind her eyes. She felt her body go limp.

*"Melanie!"*

The pain ricocheted inside her skull, taking her over completely. She wanted to bring her hands to her head, but they wouldn't move. Her legs wouldn't obey her either. Melanie tried to open her eyes, to lift herself off the concrete, but she couldn't. Nothing was working. The red of her inner vision shimmered into blue. Then purple. Then black.

Peter watched from his place next to Jenna as Melanie backed up, then began running hard toward the little trampoline.

"Should they be doing that on the concrete?" Jenna asked. "It doesn't seem very safe."

Peter shrugged. He'd have answered, but he didn't even know what to say to her anymore. How could Jenna have kept a secret like being in love with Miguel del Rios for two whole years? The fact that Miguel apparently wasn't available didn't do much to take the edge off Peter's hurt feelings, either. He was trying not to think about the trip he'd be making after school—the one to return the heart-shaped bracelet and get Chris's money back—when Melanie hit the trampoline. *I hope that bracelet's returnable*, he thought, sick at the idea that he might be stuck with it.

The crowd cheered as the petite cheerleader sailed up through the air. But something was wrong. Was Melanie supposed to be flipping so soon, so low? Her legs came out of the tuck too early and her feet glanced off hips at the rear of the pyramid, sliding forward along the cheerleaders' backs instead of landing on top of them. Peter watched in horror as Melanie struggled unsuccessfully for balance. She was going down.

"Melanie!" he shouted, bursting out of the crowd and beginning to run. She was falling—he'd never make it in time. *Oh please, oh please, oh please . . .* Her head hit the pavement with a thud so violent Peter felt it vibrate up through his shoes. "*Melanie!*"

The crowd surged in behind him as the other cheerleaders scrambled out of the pyramid. Peter dove to his knees beside the small, motionless body on the concrete, praying that she was all right. Melanie's eyes were closed, her hair fanned out around her head. Peter felt for a pulse, but his hands were shaking uncontrollably and his own heart was beating so wildly he couldn't feel anything else.

"Melanie, can you hear me?" he whispered. "Please, Melanie . . ."

A shoe nudged him from behind. The crowd was pushing in so tightly that Peter could barely see sky. "Back up!" he barked, trying to take control of the situation. "Give us some room to breathe!"

The crowd took a half-step backward, and somehow Tanya Jeffries managed to squeeze in at his side. "Oh no," she whispered, her expression shaken. "Is she . . . ?"

"Find a phone. Call 911."

Tanya nodded, then lurched to her feet. "Does anyone have a cell phone?"

"I do!" yelled a voice at the back of the crowd.

"We need an ambulance! Call 911!" Tanya shouted urgently, pushing her way toward the phone.

Melanie hadn't moved. Peter lifted one still hand off the pavement and squeezed it between his own, willing her to open her eyes, to twitch a finger, to do *something*.

*Please, God,* he prayed. *Don't let her die. Please, don't let her die.*

He stroked Melanie's forehead, smoothing her hair on the cold gray pavement. She looked so small somehow, so helpless without that hard-edged smile. Impulsively he stripped off his sweatshirt and wadded it into a ball, intending to lift her head onto his makeshift pillow. His fingers slid gently through her silky hair until they ran into something wet, something warm. Peter froze, then slowly withdrew his hand. Melanie was bleeding.

"Back up! I want all you people to back up right now!" a man's voice commanded. The crowd actually made some room as Mr. Adams, a science teacher, pushed his way toward the center with Ms. Carson at his side.

"What's happened?" Ms. Carson called out. "Who's hurt?" A chorus of confused voices tried to answer.

"One at a time!" Mr. Adams shouted. The two teachers broke through the crowd and looked down on Melanie and Peter.

"Oh, my God!" Ms. Carson whispered. Peter glanced up at the teachers' startled faces, then down at Melanie's blood on his fingers.

Crouching on Melanie's other side, Mr. Adams snatched up her wrist and felt for a pulse. Ms. Carson knelt beside him, making small, fearful noises. "I swear they didn't tell me. I didn't even know they were doing this today. . . ."

A whistle shrilled through the quad. "Out! Everyone clear the quad!" Peter recognized Coach Davis's game-day bellow. "Come on, now! You're not helping anyone by getting in the way." Some other, less powerful voices joined in to reinforce the coach's, and Peter realized that the teachers were coming out of the building in force now.

Then, very faint, very far away, Peter heard the first plaintive wail of a siren.

"Melanie," he whispered, bending low to her ear. "Melanie, can you hear me? Just squeeze my hand if you can. Squeeze my hand a little, all right?"

Nothing. The siren was growing louder.

Principal Kelly materialized out of nowhere. "How is she?" he asked anxiously.

Mr. Adams shrugged. "I don't know."

"Here, you. What's your name?"

"Peter Altmann."

"Okay, Peter. You can go. We'll take it from here."

Peter held his ground. "I want to stay."

"There's nothing you can do for her. Besides, here comes the ambulance—look."

Coach Davis and his whistle worked overtime to wave students out of the way as a gleaming white ambulance ran up onto the quad and rolled toward them over the concrete. The siren had been cut, but the lights on top still flashed erratically, eerie in the daylight. Peter gave Melanie's unresponsive hand one last squeeze, willing his strength into her. Then, as the paramedics bustled in with a backboard and a flurry of questions, he rose to his feet and backed away. The crowd of students was thick behind him, preventing him from retreating very far. Drawn, frightened faces filled his vision.

"How far did she fall?" a paramedic barked.

"How long has she been out?"

"Who's notifying her parents?"

Peter heard the questions, but not the answers, until: "Who's riding to the hospital?"

"I am!" he cried, rushing forward again. "I'm riding with her."

Melanie was on the stretcher now. The big double doors at the back of the ambulance gaped wide as the paramedics loaded her in. Before anyone could stop him, Peter jumped up behind the stretcher, sliding all the way inside.

"Hey!" Principal Kelly objected, sticking his head in through the doors.

"Let him go," a paramedic urged. "Sometimes they respond better to a friend."

The way the man said "they" sent a shiver up Peter's neck.

The principal nodded and withdrew his head, and another medic climbed in quickly on Melanie's other side. The doors banged shut. The siren shrieked to life.

"Hang on, Melanie," Peter whispered, taking her hand again. "You've got to hang in there now."

With a jolt that knocked him sideways, the ambulance sped out of the quad.

**Find out what happens next in Clearwater Crossing #3, _Heart & Soul_.**

# About the Author

Laura Peyton Roberts holds an M.A. in English literature from San Diego State University. A native Californian, she resides with her husband in San Diego.